A Flatland Fable takes place during a single day in Eckley, a small flat town in the middle of a vast flat midwestern landscape. Our protagonist is Horgan, who, at 40, is waiting—waiting for life to happen to him. And in the course of this single day, it does.

"This novel establishes Coomer as one of our most talented young writers. If *A Flatland Fable* has a moral, it could be this: Even in the dullest of places, unexpected and wonderful things can happen. . . . Coomer brings Eckley to life with a loving eye for detail, an original, dry humor, and a strong sense of story and rhythm. Written to a human scale, this fable is absorbing, astonishing, and lovely."
—*Publishers Weekly*

"Coomer in *Flatland*, like Larry McMurtry and John Updike in their early works, is a master of lyric brevity . . . [and] a vital new voice in American fiction. . . . The 'truth' Joe Coomer brings in his wonderfully crafted new novel is that there is change, surprise, evolution, and regeneration in life, even if that life is lived in a 'far, flat place' where nothing spectacular ever seems to happen. Bobbie Ann Mason and Raymond Carver have similar cautionary tales to tell. But even so, Coomer puts a peculiar spin on the ball, and pitches his own game. He makes a beautiful and complex thing from simple at-hand stuff."
—*Texas Observer*

Also by Joe Coomer

The Decatur Road

Kentucky Love

JOE COOMER

A FLAT- LAND FABLE

McGRAW-HILL BOOK COMPANY

New York St. Louis San Francisco
Toronto Hamburg Mexico

for Heather

Reprinted by arrangement with Texas Monthly Press, Inc.

First McGraw-Hill Paperback edition, 1987

1 2 3 4 5 6 7 8 9 A R G A R G 8 7

ISBN 0-07-012629-1

LIBRARY OF CONGRESS CATALOGING-IN-PUBLICATION DATA

Coomer, Joe.
 A flatland fable.
 I. Title. II. Title: Flat land fable.
[PS3553.O574F5 1987]   813'.54   87-4219
ISBN 0-07-012629-1 (pbk.)

- 1 -

The land for miles around is a level spot, flat ground.
It is just waiting for something to happen. There has
been an ice age, and a sea, a couple of tropical
jungles, a forest or two, and so on, but now there is
just the flatness with some grass, a little range brush,
and an occasional rock. There is very little or nothing
going on at all. A boy, maybe. A good long slow rain
wouldn't hurt.

The land for miles around is a baseball field. Carry
a home plate with you and you can stop anywhere,
plug it in, and begin play, hit away. There are the
cracks in the earth to contend with, bad hops, but
also the big blue sky for the ball to rise into and drop
out of. And you can run then. You can do this in the
meantime, while it's still flat.

The sun comes up in the morning here. That's
something. You can wait up for it. It comes up,
happens, early in the morning; there's nothing to
stop it; it's one of the first things, really. What it's
like: like something faraway coming to your moment, like something you knew was going to happen
all along, sure, but Christ, here it is.

A fly, not incessantly, but buzzing against the
rusted screen of the window near your bed. A fly just
waking up. And the one white sheet, because it's hot

even at night, crumpled across your brown stomach. The one fly buzzes and bangs into the screen again, and walks a little, and then buzzes off into the high, open room. And since it's morning and it's the summer and hot still, you watch him. He flies around and around the open room, under the suspended light fixture, around and around. He comes home to the screen after a while and you see there is still the morning happening outside, where it is flat.

Sometimes it is the morning, the sun, coming up from among the brush and dust in the east, and sometimes it is just the Burlington-Northern. The Northern is quicker but the sun has a more general effect. With the sun, almost every summer morning, there is an eclipse; after the greying, the subtle wearing and chafing of the edge of the earth, the edge turns orange for an instant and then brims, catches on fire: all that dry grass, hair and fur hung on barbed wire, blown grain from the long-haul trucks out on the Route, it all catches fire, just the border of the sun rimming the earth for a moment and those solar flames caught among the dryness here. People wake up early and call the Fire Department. "The whole east end of the world is on fire," they say, "and it's coming this way." The Fire Department, if he is awake, tells them he doesn't have enough water to put out the sun.

The Burlington-Northern comes west out of the night on some of the highest ground in this country. The tracks rest on a full eleven inches of gravel and crosstie. People get up on them and put their hand to their brow, like they're standing on the rim of the Grand Canyon. They feel like they can see forever, till the earth bends out from underneath their stare. The train tracks come west with Route 50 and a line of telephone poles. Between the tracks and the road there is a ditch, in case anything should ever happen, like rain. The ditch is the very lowest place in this country. There are rumors, theories, that suggest if there was enough water in the ditch, enough to keep it running, the water would make it all the way to the Gulf of Mexico, the ocean. But this would require a degree of slope almost unimaginable to most. It would require the term "downhill." Most people continue to park their trucks in neutral. Some have even gone so far as to take a glass of tap water out to the ditch and pour it in, delighting in its equidistant spread, flowing as far north, south, and west as it does east, before it is swallowed by the red dirt and dust, or taken almost momentarily and wholly up into the dry sky. "Look," the people say, pointing down at the flat earth, "isn't this the best goddamn country for baseball you ever saw?"

The sun comes up out of the brush huge and round and orange, its yellow through the earth's red dust, cool to stare at and lukewarm to the touch. It rubs you on the forehead first, the heat does, as you lean from the bed and look out. It comes up fast till it rests a foot or so above the horizon, where it's hard to look at, and hard to judge, without the earth there next to it. It moves only slowly, imperceptibly, then, through the rest of the day; no clouds to mark it by, just the open blue sky, so consistently blue it could be overcast.

Out in the red dirt, amid the morning, there is Sickopoose, the center fielder, and his mom. Sickopoose, with his back to the sun, balances on the balls of his feet and smacks his fist into the palm of his glove. His mom tosses the ball high into the air, lets it fall, and smacks a low hard line drive in Sickopoose's general direction. Sickopoose kicks out across the plowed field, leaps across the furrows, and dives, stretched taut, horizontal, screaming. He thuds into the earth, jackknives, crumples in the dust, and the ball, tipped, rolls along a furrow beyond him. It lies there, the ball does, dusted, but round and white and perfect in the V of the furrow, still. Sickopoose brings himself slowly to his knees, rests his open glove on his thigh, and looks at the perfect ball beyond him. Then he looks for the sun, which is still low in the morning, and gets up, throws the baseball in a high arc back to his mom. It plops and nestles into the soft dirt six inches from her foot.

You roll back into the bed from looking out the window, where the fly is frantic with the coming heat. The sun is blinding off the white siding of the house. You turn back over, crumpling the sheet, and there is your wife beside you, new and young and almost unexpected, gorgeous and fresh in the morning, hair down across her cheek and falling between her breasts. She is still asleep, the sheet across her white hip. And so you roll back over, leaning on your elbow. And the fly is gone. He must have found the hole in the screen, the hole just above the eyehook, where you put a screwdriver through once when you were locked out. Almost every screen in the house has these holes.

The chickens are up and moving around the yard, walking as if their legs were Popsicle sticks. They strut and peck cautiously around the old hen who sits on her brood under the corner of the garage. She fluffs and coddles. The rooster, a big, arrogant bird, moves center backyard and cackles, then spreads his useless wings and crows. He turns around and crows again and again. You sigh with him and his old hen. You had always thought that no matter how bad things got you could always fall back on the statement that you could do anything a chicken could do, and maybe do it better.

The Burlington-Northern, a little late this morning, hauls past, one hundred and eight green and yellow cars long, on its way to the Eckley Elevator in Eckley. Big trucks, carrying grain too, run alongside on the Route. And the grain—oats, wheat, rye—falls through cracks in the trailers, through the rusted seams of the cars, and falls along the Route and between the rails, and blows. The wind comes, but it doesn't rain, hasn't rained.

Witherspoon, the catcher, four-foot-eight and ninety-five pounds, a doorstop, corners a calf in the corral. He locks the calf's mother in a pen, picks up his catcher's mitt, pounds it with his calloused fist, and steps between the calf and its mother. The calf, strung, bawling, paces back and forth, looking for an opening. Witherspoon settles to his haunches, squats in the manure dust in front of the calf, pounds his mitt again, and waits. Wide-eyed the calf darts and Witherspoon shifts, half-hops to the side, a cutting horse, and jams his glove up in front of the calf's pink nose. The calf backs up and shoots for the other side, but Witherspoon sidles again, raising dust and squaring his shoulders in front of the calf. They go at it, again and again, grunting and snorting, the calf pivoting and racing for a gap and Witherspoon prancing sideways on his haunches, squatting, his mitt up, his toes bent deep into the manure, knocking down errant throws, wild pitches. Nothing will get by him. But the sun rises up over the second rail of the corral, and from the house, Witherspoon's dad calls him in to breakfast.

You know one of the last of the long summer days has come, is coming. A dust devil twirls in the backyard, picking up feathers and straw, whips around the edge of the house, and returns and falls apart before your eyes. The fly is back too, trying to get back through the hole in the screen. You put your finger there for a moment to thwart him. You roll back into the bed, feel the muscles strain around your heart, a little twinge.

How is your dying father?

"Morning, Horgan," she says, reaching over and rubbing your belly. You remember her, almost afraid that it's not true, but yes, she's here. God.

"Hi. Morning," Horgan whispers.

"How're you feeling?" she asks, and drops her hand under the white sheet.

"I'm okay, I'm good. I think I can."

"Love you."

And Horgan, moves to her, quietly, holding your breath, in the morning.

Everything in Eckley, the center of this country, is galvanized. Things come that way. From the air the town looks like a great many chicken feeders and overturned buckets. The whole place is corrugated and bumps when you run your hand along it: roofs, water tanks and towers, the grain elevator, every windmill, every barn. In the middle of the day, sun glaring, a tin roof or door will flash at you like a shard of glass under your fingernail. But in the morning and evening the whole town is the color of the sky. Shake this town, it sounds like thunder. Let a wind come and it whistles. And the tin roofs, they're for when the rain arrives: to hear the first startling pop, and then the drop's slow course down the tin furrow. This town listens for rain like a bucket: mouth open, waiting.

A sweat already billowing from his forehead, Gaspar, pitcher for this evening's game, wakes up. His fingers grope for the baseball he meant to clutch all night long, and finally they find it underneath his backbone. He kicks away the sheet, rolls out, and then strips the bed, shoves the mattress to the floor, and yanks the box spring from the bed frame. It's all he can do to get it up on edge and ride it down the narrow staircase to the back door. Outside, he leans it up against the house, marks out a generous strike zone with a can of red spray paint, and then back to the house, where he dresses, picks up his bag of baseballs, tennis balls, oranges, and horseapples, an assortment, and takes his Flintstone vitamin. At the back door he adjusts the visor of his cap. He steps out, steps to the box spring, steps off the paces, makes a line in the red dirt with his toe. And he begins, the spilled bag of balls and fruit at his feet, winding up and uncoiling, zip, pop, throwing them everything he's got.

Across town the Rutley twins, right and left field, stand up close to the house, almost under the eave, and toss the hardball, hookstyle, up on the roof where they can't see it. Then listen for its tin smack and gathering roll, positioning themselves, gloves up, and fighting for the ball's fall off the roof. They manage this twenty-three times before their father raises the bedroom window, sticks his bedraggled tin head out, and yells, "You twins cut that out. It's all day before that ball game starts," and bangs the window to.

Horgan lifts himself gently out and off of her and

collapses at her side. She rolls and throws a leg over his thigh.

"That was good," she breathes.

"Right," Horgan wheezes back.

"Maybe again at lunch," she says.

"Don't know," he blows.

"Well, after supper for sure."

"Got the ball game tonight," he suggests.

"We'll see, though," she says, "after the ball game. I just can't get over the idea that anytime we do it, that time could be the baby."

Horgan's mind crawls under the bed. He knows she is going to bring up the doctor again.

"I'm going this afternoon to see the doctor. I'm late. It might already be," she says.

"You've been late ever since you got off the pill. Six times." His mind sneaks out from underneath the foot of the bed, bellies to the closet, and throws some dirty clothes over itself.

"That's something else, honey. You know what the doctor said. If I'm still not pregnant, and he'll know today, we should both go in and get ourselves checked over. It's sort of like Little League, you know, bottom of the sixth." She puts in a "ha, ha" after that last one. Then notices his mind is hiding. "But we'll talk about it after the appointment. No sense worrying ahead of having to. Right?"

"Right," Horgan affirms, sheepishly dragging a foul pair of underwear off his mind's face.

Feeb, shortstop, breaking in a new glove, looking for an unimaginable stab, dips it in the used oil drum at Phillips 66. He has only the one day, ten hours or so, to get it as soft as his own pink hand. He walks back home, his glove black and dripping on the sidewalk like a nosebleed, and since he hasn't an old

Indian woman to gnaw on it, he steals his dad's truck keys and runs over the glove again and again, grinding gears.

Route 50 runs in one ear of Eckley and out the other. It spends no time at all there, really. There's not a blinking yellow light or even a sign that says "SLOW—ECKLEY." The highway moves straight, fast, and flat through the town, like the place isn't there at all, like it's just more dry country to get through, the same old thing. The Burlington-Northern has a single spur, to the elevator, but generally moves through pretty quickly itself. And the telephone poles, they let down a single strand, a loose thread, and keep right on going. One of these days someone is going to stop, by chance or circumstance, the world coming around, and the people here are going to pounce on him like a Messiah.

What there is in Eckley, and the reason to stop, is the Eckley Elevator, the reason the trucks and train slow down, the town's here, and the telephone even bothers to ring. It, the elevator, rises without comparison on this flat place, concrete canisters, like a whale breaching on a calm sea. The biggest thing around, taking in the least: grain—chaff, dust, and seed of all the summer and spring—gorging itself on cereal stuffs. The birds—sparrow, quail, crow—flutter and gawk about the elevator as if it were dead on the beach. The lone and level sands stretch far away.

The old woman, Miss Marian Eckley, she spends her free moments spreading poison for the birds. She moves willfully through the galvanized bins and hoppers of her elevator, under the chutes and all the way around the huge canisters, the tiny white pellets heaped in her uplifted apron, and she clucks while she casts them across the ground. A bird, descending in slow circles out of the morning and the orange reflection off the bins, stalls and settles in front of her. It ruffles, slants its brown head, and looks at her, a deep curious pupil. And though it takes an effort, the bird far away and cautious, she tosses, gently, a few pellets its way.

How is your dying father?

It is warm now, so Horgan flips his pillow to the cool side. He looks out the window again and sees the morning is well on its way. What else could happen this day? There would be breakfast, and work, and lunch, and that, maybe, and then to see his dad, and then the ball game, and that again, perhaps, if he could, and maybe that would be all. Just so much palaver and nibbling, and that, till the day was through, waiting for a baby, waiting for his father, for a fire. Maybe it will rain. Maybe we will be rained out this evening. That's a possibility for hope.

He wishes, suddenly, that he had the authority to set her, Miss Eckley, to set her about collecting a full quart of gnat's milk. Putting his hand on the small of her back and pointing out a likely swarm, giving her a smile and nod of encouragement.

"Horgan," Kidder says again, coming out of the bathroom with a towel held tightly between her thighs so that she has to take baby duck steps, "here's your vitamin." She hands him a glass of water and a pill that reminds him of the knob on the end of a baseball bat. She's been bringing them out of the bathroom every morning for the past six months.

"I'm not seventy," he'd said the first time, "I've been doing all right," and he'd put a hurt look on his bottom lip and part of his chin. "I'm only fourteen years older than you are."

"It's for the baby, honey," she'd said, "I know you're not even forty-one yet. You're real good. It's for the baby. I take one too." And she reached down and rubbed herself with the towel, her legs bowed, as if she was a cello.

He'd never tried to have kids before, it was true, but he thought he could. They'd only been trying for six months now. Still, the vitamins aren't a great boost to his ego. They're a prop. He wants to do it on his own. And then there is the other thing that doesn't help: for the last two months, as soon as they finish, every time, Kidder spins around on the bed, raises herself up on her shoulder blades and props her feet high up on the wall. Horgan knows it's so everything will run downhill. She stays that way for a full five minutes, making small talk, before she goes to the bathroom for the towel and vitamin.

Across Eckley the morning is an orange blanket shaken out. The wind picks up the dust and lint, funnels them about, changes things a little from yesterday. The shadows of houses go all the way down the street.

Yanks, batting cleanup, out in the middle of the asphalt street, pops the ball up in the air with his left hand and hauls back, folding himself up into a two-inch strike zone, and then explodes at the ball, like a deck of cards pinched and let go; arms, bat, cap, legs, go in all directions, but the ball leads out high, white, and true down the street, finally falling and caroming off the steel cab of a pickup and then rolling further down the street along the curb. Yanks crouches in fear, a manhole in the street, a dent in the truck more than plausible. But no one wakes up. No one comes out. He stands up, drops the bat brazenly on the street, raises his arms in Homeric glory, and trundles around the bases—mailbox, curb, fender—nodding his head, yes, yes, it's true, again.

The sun chases the night across the county and through Eckley and out west, and the night leaves shadows like cuts, like pieces of the past. They heal to noon and then relapse. The day is a bleeder. It happens over and over again.

"Horgan," Kidder calls from the kitchen, "time to get up. Just a half-day today, remember."

Horgan moves his mind around and remembers, yes, it's Saturday, just a half-day at the station. That's okay. No one had called during the night. He looks back out the window, winks at another dust devil to see if that will stop it, and wishes the wind would die down. That wouldn't help matters if something, God grant it, were to happen. He rolls on the bed, sits up, snatches a sleepy seed from his eye and flicks it toward the throw rug, where it won't be easily spotted. Then he rises, popping on his underwear, popping the elastic in front again for his work that morning already, and patting his stomach. He puts on one of his ten blue, short-sleeved shirts with the white oval above the pocket that says "Horgan" in dark blue cursive. For a moment a slight sensation of nausea runs through him... wearing a shirt with his name on it for the sixth day in a row... but he runs that off by rubbing his crotch and remembering to pee.

He stands over the bowl. Sometimes he had to wait a bit. But it finally comes and Horgan nods, megaphones his voice, and says, "Okay, truck number three, get a hose on that second window. Careful, she's burning hot. Careful. Careful with that glass. Okay. Good. Good. She's under control. Wrap her up." And he gives himself a little shake. These outbreaks, they broke up the meantime. Maybe it will rain, he thinks again. Maybe we will be saved.

"Horgan," Kidder calls, "what are you doing?"

"Making water, honey," he yells back.

Norblunk and his little brother, outfielders both, broken arms both, are propped up on the couch by their mother and watch the Saturday morning cartoons. They were on the same bicycle that, hitting a curb, went no further. The boys did. Norblunk the older says to Norblunk the younger, "You can still throw, can't you?"

"Yep."

"Well, I can still catch."

But the sky is clear blue after the orange. The Dairy Mart on the Route blinks, blinks, and blinks again, its lights blinking off to the day. The manager tapes a sign to the inside of the glass door, "Before and After the Game—Dairy Mart."

On the corner of the Route and Main Street the pump man at Phillips 66 finds someone has been messing with his used oil. The drips lead off down the street. He scratches his head and then has to wipe his head with a rag. To his flat tire billboard he attaches the cardboard sign he made up the night before: "GO ECKLEY." Then figures, apparently, what's the use? and takes the sign back down.

But maybe it will rain, he thinks, thinking it into the ground. What they say: if you don't like the weather here just wait a minute. "Honey," Horgan calls, yelling to the kitchen through the hallway, "maybe it will rain today."

"Fat chance, Coach," Kidder yanks out from underneath him. "That's not what the radio says. Hot and windy and dry, it says," she says, kicking him across the linoleum.

Young Whit, consummate, precise, without the least bit of hesitation, practices the bench. Elbows on knees, chin in hand, he sits on the back porch steps waiting to play right field for an inning late in the game. He practices cinching his bowels, because with all his free time he drinks too much water from the cooler. Game time is still nine hours away, but he's already dressed, ready, his glove on the concrete step next to his broad butt, his cap pulled down tightly on his burr, folding his ears over. He trains his eye by watching the birds swoop across the sky of his backyard. For him there's just the time in between.

The Burlington-Northern pulls a long freight into the Eckley Elevator and runs into Miss Eckley on the loading dock. It's the train that bounces back. The elevator foreman stands at her side, rubbing the inside of his forearms.

"Yes, ma'am," he says.

"And as soon as the cars are loaded," she says, not even looking at him, but pointing, "get them out of here, and get the trucks in and unloaded. We've got three days of work to get done today. I want it done."

"Yes, ma'am. We're due for an inspection today, though. We're scheduled with Horgan for today. All this business the dust will be high. He might cite us."

"I'll manage the Fire Department."

"He'll squawk."

"Get this work done."

"Yes, ma'am."

And she turns toward the office, stops to yank an unlit cigarette from a man's face and stamp on it— "You damn fool, inspection today"—and the whole elevator shudders as the hoppers and chutes start up, and Miss Eckley slams her galvanized door.

"Oh, boy," Horgan glees, "oatmeal for breakfast," and he hugs Kidder, bends down and buries his nose between her breasts and rubs. "The oats are just flying everywhere this morning," he adds. He sits down at the table, next to her, and plunges a brimming spoonful into his mouth.

"It's hot, Horgan," she says, over the whooshing sound the air makes as he zeros his lips and sucks in huge drafts.

"Okay—WHOOSH—honey—WHOOSH—got to—WHOOSH—replenish—WHOOSH—myself," and he swallows.

She hands him a piece of toast with wheat germ sprinkled over it.

"Thanks, honey."

"Much work to do today?" she asks.

"No. Inspection out at the elevator."

"Be careful out there. Don't let her be bossy."

"I won't," he says. "Gonna talk to her about the boys' fathers too."

"When will you see your dad?"

"I'll have a couple free hours after lunch, before the pre-game practice. You want to go with me? You can see the doctor then." His mind throws this in behind his back. He shivers.

"No, I've got to go in this evening. The tests won't be in till then."

"You're gonna miss the game?"

"Just part of it. Just the first part. I'll stop in on your dad too while I'm there. He'll have two visits today."

"He sure loves you."

"I know," she says.

"He keeps talking about my mother."

"I know," she says.

"When I was young I thought it would stop. But it hasn't."

"I know."

"He's still, really, just waiting for her to come back."

"I know, honey."

"I wish he would stop it."

"I know," she says.

"I sure love you."

"I know, Horgan."

"I hope the test is okay."

"It will be. I feel funny. Like the whole world is going to bust open. Eat your oatmeal."

"It's good," he says, "it's not hot anymore. It's just right. We're going to get creamed tonight."

"Maybe you won't."

"Maybe we'll get killed."

"Maybe the boys will surprise you. That other team has the long bus ride to deal with."

"I just wish the whole town wasn't so sure we're gonna get creamed."

"Well, honey, you've lost to them seven years running. They've got four times the number of boys to make a good team. Springtown is four times the size of Eckley."

"You know, this is the first year I've ever had someone extra to sit on the bench," Horgan adds.

"See?" she says, bless her heart.

"Yeah, but I just keep waiting. One of these years…" And Horgan falters, a spoonful of oatmeal in his cheek, "Maybe it will rain."

"What's the use?" Pillsneck wants to know anyway.

"Coach said to practice, Pillsneck. Me and you, we're supposed to slide into these chickens. Now come on."

"Coach is a pork sword," Pillsneck says.

"You're a pork sword."

"We're gonna get killed, my dad says so."

"Aw, your dad's just mad cause you gotta play first base and don't get to pitch."

"Well, I'm a better pitcher than Gaspar, and Coach knows it."

"You pitched last game. It's Gasp's turn."

"Aw," and Pillsneck throws his open hand at Shrugsby.

"Aw, yourself," Shrugsby says, and turns away, leads off, careful, careful, scratching back a little dirt in the chicken yard, and then sees his chance and flies, scratching out, digging in and running, running hard to within ten feet of a big rooster and then hitting the loose ground, hard on the haunches, and skidding into him, dust, dirt, feather, boy, cloud of earth, and squawking, till all clears and Shrugsby looks around himself, pushes up, brushes his pant legs and mumbles, "Safe."

"Yer out," Pillsneck crows at the other end.

"Pork sword!" Shrugsby screams.

"Pork sword breath!" screams Pillsneck.

"Aw," Shrugsby moans, turning away again, looking for another chicken.

There is dust and wind everywhere in this country and all over Eckley and the day still beginning, stretching out over the flatness.

And then the red phone rings, the red one next to

the black one on the kitchen wall, and Horgan is up, turning over his chair and oatmeal on the way. He answers it, says "yes," three times quickly and then, "Coming as fast as I can; wait on me," and Kidder runs after him through the hall and living room and screams, "Be careful," just as the front door slams to. Horgan runs along the yellow curb in front of his house and jumps on the fire engine parked there, jams his index finger and thumb into the ignition before he remembers the key is in his pocket, but then he's off, lights flashing in the early morning, sirens blaring, his heart out in front of him, bouncing on the red hood.

- 2 -

He had never wanted, when he was a kid, to grow up to be a fireman. The notion hadn't hit him till he was almost thirty-three. It was the fall, and he was out in the front yard with his dad, burning a pile of leaves and brush. The leaves were brown and yellow and made a blue smoke, and the limbs cracked and collapsed, and it was the first day of the season that needed a sweater. The smell was from some place ancient and holy and sensual and reminded him of his past faintly. It brought tears to his eyes, and he'd told his dad the truth, said it was just the smoke.

That had given him the idea. He found himself hunting things to burn around the house, just for the smoke and the beauty of the fire. These, and the warmth. He'd take off his jacket or coat and get as close as he could, at times singeing his eyebrows or the hair on his forearms. Doing these things for the joy and sight of it, till later that winter it became something else for him, something opposite, making it bigger somehow, making him want to devote himself to it. There were two old stacks of rotting lumber in the backyard. He'd set them both on fire and stood back to watch. The flames pulsed, then rose, and just as a few of the old boards began to collapse a field mouse ran out from underneath one of the stacks and straight across to the other stack, into a bed of red coals. He moved, Horgan did, crouching, not knowing what to do, listening to the mouse screech. Finally he picked up a board and, knocking away some of the lumber, scraped the mouse out of the coals onto the grass. He knew it was a mistake as soon as he'd done it. He bent down, saw and smelled the singed fur, the black and curled paws, saw that the mouse was blind. It rolled twice and ended up on its haunches, shaking. Horgan thought he should go ahead and kill it: the awful squeaking it made; but he couldn't; he sat there with him, bent down over and around him, and forgot the fires, waited on his haunches, his heart pounding, till the mouse died a half hour later.

So then it became the horror as well as the joy and depth of it for him, the warmth and pain. He put the mouse in a corner of the backyard where the grass was high.

And then, before he had even thought about it specifically, before he'd even had a chance to wait on it, something happened. Eckley's only paid fireman died in his sleep. Horgan woke up and heard the news from his father, a town councilman: there had been a small dust explosion at the Eckley Elevator during the night and old man Dinks, twenty-five years on the job, had been killed trying to save a man trapped inside one of the bins. A huge chunk of concrete had broken loose and crushed him, driven him like a spike a good twelve feet down into the grain. That morning, after they'd dug up Dinks, Miss Eckley started rebuilding, and Horgan applied for the Fire Department opening.

His was the only application. None of the regular volunteer firemen wanted the job because it paid only a little more than what it cost for one human to live, and because the job required an overly abundant amount of plain waiting. There were barely enough people in Eckley to set enough fires to keep things interesting. If there were two calls a week people started talking arson. Paramedics from the hospital took emergency calls, the Sheriff's Department handled wrecks, natural disasters were infrequent, and every house in town now had city water, a water hose in both the front and back yards. The Burlington-Northern always set a few grass fires along the tracks, but good, steady firefighter work just wasn't often offered. It was a job of inspections, making sure fire extinguishers were topped up, giving a program for the elementary school every year.

So he applied, lying about his height, saying he was a good five-seven and three-quarters, even though he was only five-five and a half, detailing his experiences as an enlisted man (a boom operator), and a caboose rider for the Burlington. He thought about the blank space for further remarks, about the afternoon of burning leaves and the morning of the mouse, but he didn't put these down. Instead he noted his desperate need for work, that there wasn't any work in Eckley for an able-bodied man if he didn't want to work for Miss Eckley, and that he was tired of sitting around.

And he wouldn't have gotten the job if his father hadn't been on the council, been the mayor that term. Miss Eckley, through a series of telephone calls the afternoon after the explosion, tried to abolish the Eckley Fire Department. That evening, at an open council meeting, she stood at the far end of the junior high school lunch room and traded shouts with Horgan's father. Tiny and sharp everywhere but for her great motherly bosom, sixty years old, she pounded the table with her clenched fist.

"It's nepotism," she screamed.

"It's our only application," he screamed back at her.

"The position isn't needed. I pay seventy percent of the whole Department's salary myself through the elevator's taxes. We could use that money on direct fire prevention. We've got the volunteers for grass fires."

Horgan's father sat down. He turned to each of the council members, waited a moment, then said, "Boys, I know she scares you. She has always startled me. I'm retiring next year. Let's not let her take away whatever peace in sleep we've now got. You all know Horgan's a good, honest boy and that he'll do his best to protect us. She's not after what you think she is, what she says she is. On my word Horgan's a grown man and as good a man as Dinks was." And when he said "was," he looked up at Miss Eckley and laid his two palms open on the table. The Fire Department was retained, and Horgan hired, by a five to four margin.

"You can all go to hell," Miss Eckley said, railing out of the cafeteria, white from head to toe with concrete dust. She had only bothered to take a wet washcloth to the sockets of her eyes, and they bored out of the whiteness deep and black. "Out of the way," she blew, stiff-arming her way through the door. She walked like a sawblade into the night, her elbows, knees, and chin carbide tipped.

And so Horgan began his days. He continued to live in his father's house on Third Street (there is no Fourth Street and the backyard stretches out to the Mississippi), but painted the curb out front a bright yellow and stenciled "Fire Dept." in two places.

A FLATLAND FABLE

Since he was the only fireman he began driving the fire engine home in the evening, and everywhere else he went. He had a hotline phone installed in the house and a CB on the truck so he could be found twenty-four hours a day. He didn't want to miss out on anything.

In his spare duty time he participated in charity and civic activities. For Muscular Dystrophy he stood out alone on Route 50 with his rubber boot in supplication. For the Bicentennial he and the third grade of Eckley Elementary painted four of the five fireplugs in town red, white, and blue and of the fifth they made a tiny Uncle Sam: canvas trousers, a pink cherubic face with a three-quarter-inch nut for a nose. For spite, and in good sense, he painted a yellow streak of fire lanes in front of the Elementary and Middle School, eliminating the teachers' best parking spaces. That was for the old times, though he realized as he painted that only one of his old teachers was still active. But he had waited twenty-three years for his chance and he wasn't going to give it up for reason's sake. It would take more than that. For the pure ego of it he drove the engine in every parade that would have him, carrying at odd times the town council, the cub scout troop, the candy stripers from the hospital, and one great November evening the homecoming queen. Kidder was a member of her court, the third runner-up, and though Horgan addressed her once with a sweep of his arm, a glance, and the words "Hey, girls," she didn't pay another bit of attention to him. It broke his heart, she was so beautiful, but it passed. The next morning he was putting on one of the blue shirts with his name on it like always. He hardly thought of her for the next five years.

And then there are the fires.

And it's true, a relatively great deal of grass burns around Eckley. The fires are almost always associated with either the Route or the Burlington-Northern, a cigarette butt from a car or a cinder from the train, and so will burn black half-moons out from the road or tracks. If it is the summer, and it always seems to be the summer, there's little to burn because everything has already dried up and blown away, and Horgan is almost ashamed to turn on the lights and siren for the few faint flames he finds when he arrives. He usually doesn't even waste the water, walks around with a wet burlap sack and beats on the burning earth. Then, after the fire is out, he looks for rabbit holes and artifacts in the cleared ground. He shuffles about, hands in pockets, and kicks at bottle necks and mounds of dirt. That is what makes the grass fires worthwhile, that, and the smell of the smoke. It makes him want to fall asleep and run at the same time.

And then there are the grass fires that seem to come from nowhere, that start in the middle of a field, and if the wind isn't blowing, grow into a sort of three-dimensional reflection of an eclipse, black smoking center with a burning ring. If the wind blows and it's early summer, when the grass is dry but still thick Horgan always hits the town emergency whistle on his way out so the volunteers will come. The horn blows a long steady air raid blast and Horgan lets them know where he's going by the radio. The volunteers usually arrive four or five minutes after Horgan, bedraggled and angry, or more often, jobraggled and excited. They're either pulling on clothes or pulling them off. They work on the fires together then, yelling, riding herd on the flames with the truck and hose, cutting barbed wire so they can pass through. Horgan is so happy to have a team that he's actually depressed when the fire is out, the hayfield or house saved. It's what eventually led him to coach the Eckley Little League team. He likes the shouting, the bustle, his active role, the passage of time without his notice.

And of other than the grass fires there is very little. An occasional skillet of bacon flaring up, a carburetor belching, a false alarm from Whit's lumberyard almost twice a week.

Whit, the boy, is Horgan's bench warmer because he has an intense habit of standing staunchly motionless at the plate as pitches whiz by him. The boy can field fairly well, and has a barrel chest, strong arms, and a wide girth from working in his dad's lumberyard, but he just doesn't seem to want to swing at the ball, so Horgan plays him in the field for an inning or two, and takes his strikeout as best he can.

Whit, the father, is the Fire Department's best customer. He is on the red phone to Horgan feverishly, in a sweat, at the smell or sight of smoke. Whenever any of the yard's neighbors burn their trash Whit has Horgan and his engine down there, knocking cinders out of the sky. Horgan usually drives down and lets the father stand on the truck and watch the trash burn while he goes and plays catch with the son. He does it for lack of anything else to do, and because Whit has donated the lumber for the ballfield bleachers. Horgan had suggested it one day when all three of the lumberyard's neighbors were burning trash. Horgan had called them all up that morning, the first day of the Little League season—the Phillips 66, Mrs. Jacobs, and the La Motel—and told them it was National Cleanup Day and to burn everything that would hold a match. It was good, heavy, straight yellow pine that Horgan chose for his bleachers.

The only real fire of any consequence that he'd had to battle for the past seven years was deliberately set. John Ooper, sure, but still curious, and impatient to see a little bit of what it would be like, set fire to his own home and sat out in the front yard to watch it burn. He was waiting on the apocalypse, the great conflagration. He knew the whole world was going to burn and explode; it was just a matter of time, so he did his part by drenching his carpets in gas and chunking a burning newspaper through one of the windows. Horgan and the volunteers saved the chimney, the foundation, and all the heavy metal things Ooper owned, like his bathtub and his fireplace grate. It took a three-hour stretch and half the town's water to do it. When he went to ask Ooper what had happened, Ooper precariously balanced on the curb in his laceless shoes, Ooper simply stated, "Something of what it's gonna be like when it happens. We're all marking time. We're waiting on It. Your puny hose," and Ooper simply stopped.

Horgan reached over and yanked a button off Ooper's shirt and said, "Numb nut." Then he turned back to his black-faced volunteers. Ooper, without the responsibility of keeping up a house, set up a pup tent and now waits full time.

This was almost two years ago, and other than this and the grass fires, there's just the in between time. The time between fires. There is a great deal of it. Horgan tries to fill it up with inspections, plug checks, and keeping the engine clean and ready, but still feels his life is in line at the bank, or standing in a foyer, or walking to the mailbox. He sweeps out the galvanized firehouse, constantly aware that something might occur to him, that a life in its entirety will occur to him. He chose his occupation for its combination of adventure and security, and for the smell of burning leaves, the squeak of a dying mouse. He thought the job would have something to do with saving people, but it hasn't turned out that way. There is the feeling of whistling. He has spent forty years trying not to feel this way: that all his life has been and still is a preparation for a happening that was not happening. Maybe a tornado will come, he thinks, maybe it will rain. He waits for the infernal ringing of the red phone, the passage of time without his notice.

- 3 -

Knowing just how much she'll take, Horgan wraps
the old American-LaFrance around the corner of
Third and the Route on two wheels, chunks her up
to third gear when she thuds, bouncing, back to the
pavement, and then levels his mind on speed. He
reaches down, brings his fire helmet back up and
clamps it on his head, and then two-tugs the air horn
for the rhythm of it. There is a smile on his face while
he thinks what to do next. The engine is an open
model. The wind tries to take Horgan's helmet, but
he reaches up and pulls the strap under his chin.
Yapeenahuwee! Horgan thinks. He ambles across
the double yellow line on the Route for a minute or
so as he pulls on his coat then rights her up as soon
as he's dressed. It's the snaps on the coat and the big
American-LaFrance steering wheel that make it dif-
ficult. The wheel could use two big men. Horgan's
arms are spread-eagle to manage it. He feels as if he's
holding up a placard between rounds at a boxing
match. The seat is jammed all the way forward,
under the big wheel; still Horgan can't use the back-
rest if he's to reach the three pedals: clutch, brake,
throttle, each with a 2×4 block strapped to them. He
eyes the road between the dash and the upper portion of the steering wheel. The sun stares back at him

through the same opening. Can't see, Horgan thinks. He floors her, two-tugging the air horn again for good measure, hoping all the old, deaf, and blind people aren't out yet, and that everyone else can get out of his way.

Horgan rubs his eyes with one hand then puts the sun back in them. When he sees the dirt road looming he, for lack of good brakes, jams the truck down into third, screech, down into second, screech, and then grinds the gears, as he turns the corner, back down into first. Then he opens her up again, the sun now hot on his left cheek but still green in his eyes. The red dust from the road funnels out from underneath the engine and is caught in the strong crosswind and blows through the barbed wire fence and across the fields on its way to Eckley too. He still cannot see any smoke. He thought he'd see smoke by now, and be able to judge how far gone the barn was. If he'd have any chance at all. And as he moves further down between the two barbed wire fences that decide the road in this flat place something besides the dawn begins to dawn on him. The engine slows as it nears the old Dutton place, Horgan dropping the gears with a deliberate stubbornness, his eye firmly fixed on the pristine galvanized Dutton barn, smokeless. He tries to remember exactly what the old man said on the phone. "My barn's caught fire," he'd said. "It's burning right now," he'd said. "Come right out," he'd said. Horgan thought these things would lead anybody to believe a barn was on fire. He knew the old man had only the one barn. Old Dutton was his dad's best friend, had been on the town council when Horgan was hired. He pulls the truck up between the weather-beaten house and the barn and climbs down. The two boys, Shrugsby and Pillsneck, are coming hard down from the chicken pens. Horgan goes into the open barn. Maybe the old man has put it out himself. He leans over the pipe stalls and looks into the tack room and wanders out the other end of the barn. No sign of fire. No smoke in the air. There isn't much in the barn to burn anyway. Everything is tin and oil-field pipe. The two boys have made it down into the barnyard and begin to jump up and down and yell.

"Fire," they scream, "fire, fire."

Horgan runs back through the barn, holding his helmet hard to his skull. Maybe it's the house or a field. Maybe the old man was delirious on the phone. He breaks back out into the sun among the yelling boys.

"Where?" he yells at them, grabbing Shrugsby, the old man's grandson and Horgan's second baseman, grabbing him by the shoulders and shaking him and yelling, "Where? Where?" to calm the boy.

"Where?" Shrugsby screams back at him. "Where? Where?"

"Where's the fire?" Horgan yells.

"Where is it?" Shrugsby screams, beginning to cry. The sirens are still blaring on the engine, and it is hard to hear anything. "Is Grandpa all right?" Tears are streaming down his face now as Horgan shakes him again to calm him.

"Tell me," Horgan says, "where is the fire?"

"I don't know," the boy blurbles, "we were up in the chicken pens, sliding into chickens, Coach, like you told us to."

"Well, I don't know where it is either, Shrugsby," Horgan says.

"Maybe there ain't one," Pillsneck pipes in, as if he is sick of the stupidity of everyone else in the class, and only speaks up to get things going again. It brings Horgan back to himself, and Shrugsby stops crying.

"Well, maybe," Horgan tells Pillsneck, and starts across the barnyard toward the house. "I got a phone call, though," he says. "I was called in."

While Shrugsby turns off the siren on the engine Pillsneck jumps on Horgan's heels. "Why can't I pitch today, Coach? I ought to pitch today," Pills neck says, his face gnarled and red, full of worry.

Horgan pushes him out from underneath his feet, and knocks on the old man's door. He knocks again after a moment and the old man says, "Come in, door's open, push on it."

And so Horgan does that, stepping into the kitchen, pushing Pillsneck back out from between his legs and the door with a shove in the face.

"Coach!" Pillsneck hollers, "Coach!"

"Morning, Horgan," the old man says, standing over a three-minute egg.

Horgan doesn't know what to do. He stands on the linoleum, his hands at his side. "Am I here on the wrong day, Dutton?"

"Not that I know of, Horgan. Is it a holiday?"

Horgan sits at the table. He puts the palm of one hand on his knee, and lays his other arm on the formica. "Didn't you call me about a barn fire this morning? You can get in a lot of trouble putting in a false alarm like that. I rushed all the way out here. Left my breakfast on the table."

"I didn't put in no call. Must of been somebody imitating my voice," the old man says, bringing his egg to the table. Horgan sits quietly and watches while he puts the egg on a paper towel and then cracks and peels it. The thing is, the reason is, the thing is, that this old man, Horgan thinks, has the most unimitatable voice he's ever heard. Dutton is a huge old man, still six-four after his shrinkage, and his voice comes, instead of from his socks, from about another four feet under the ground he stands on. His voice is like pushing a big oak table across a concrete floor, or ripping the bass string out of a piano and shooting arrows with it. His voice is made up of Bs and Gs, and all his words have double the consonants of everyone else's. Horgan had known him for forty years. The old man and his dad had always been friends.

After Dutton eats his egg, Horgan calls him a son of a bitch. Then he takes off his helmet and coat because he feels a little odd with them on and no fire around. Then he makes a face at Pillsneck, who still has his nose pressed against the back door window, and who is still tapping on the pane with his finger.

"Must have been one of these kids," the old man says, grating the air around him. And Horgan notices the old guy is nervous. He'd never thought that anybody with a voice that deep could get nervous.

So he says, "Can I have one of them eggs? Kidder hasn't let me eat an egg in three months."

"Think I'll have another too," Dutton answers, gouges. "Yep, must of been one of these damned kids. I'm sorry, Horgan, about your breakfast. Seems like I've been up waiting for hours. I'll get you an egg." He starts the eggs, laying them gently, for such a huge old man, in the bottom of the pot and then running the water over them, tossing in a pinch of salt. "Just a little while now," he says.

Horgan, watching the eggs, thinks they look pregnant, just like the bellies he has seen in pictures. Kidder has a whole library now on pregnancy, books and pamphlets all over the house, everywhere he turns. Women giving birth on every page. Maybe not every page. The books usually start out with pictures of happy, playing children, blocks in their hands, and jump immediately to diagrams and charts on fertility, line drawings of sperm minnowing about in a petri dish, jump again—and Horgan thinks this is an awfully big jump that the books take for granted—to pencil sketches of the fetus during each of its stages and finally to the big day, the bloody turmoil, heads emerging, and then pictures of joyously sweating women. It is almost too much. And scattered throughout, from cover to cover, are pictures of bellies: flat bellies, protruding bellies, black and white and yellow bellies, obese bellies, bellies where part of the breast got in the picture, bellies so taut Horgan has to rub his own before Kidder turns the page. The eggs did look like pregnant bellies. But so did a cement truck he'd passed yesterday. I'll be damned if anybody ever takes a picture of Kidder's belly if she gets pregnant, Horgan thinks.

The old man puts a paper towel down for Horgan, placing the egg pregnantly on it. It wobbles a little.

"I'm not hungry anymore," Horgan says. "You take mine," and he rolls the egg, calculating the arc, back across the table to Dutton.

The old man looks up at Horgan as if he might cuff him.

"Don't cuff me," Horgan says. "False alarm," he explains.

And the old guy smiles a little, and then Horgan sees the nervousness come back.

"Everything all right, Dutton?"

"I'm fine, son. How's your daddy today?"

"Going to see him this afternoon."

"He's bad, isn't he, Horgan?"

"Yes, sir, he's bad."

"Horgan, me and your daddy, we never kept a secret from one another."

"What is it? What's wrong?"

"Well, Horgan, your daddy's dying."

Horgan pushes the salt and pepper shakers around one another. "I know that, Dutty."

"Horgan, this grandson of mine, I appreciate you being good to him on that ball team. It means a lot to him. I tell him about his daddy playing ball when he was a kid so it means a lot to him to play ball."

Horgan has the feeling that he is losing grasp of the whole morning. That it is getting away from him. He says, "He's a good boy, Dutty, you've done real good with him."

"Your daddy always told you everything about your momma, didn't he?"

"Doris? Sure. He told me everything. He had to. I don't remember her at all. I was too young when she run off. But I really don't want to talk about her now. That's all Daddy does, talk about her coming back. He hasn't heard from her in thirty-nine years and that's all he talks about."

"Yes. Well, what I'm getting at Horgan, and I want your opinion on it, is this boy—and I'm ashamed to tell about it—he, I, I've never told him that his momma and daddy were both drinking that night they died on the highway. He'll find out one of these days, you know he will, and he'll reproach me for it, I know, and I'm just afraid. Do you understand that? What would you think if you were him? I'm afraid, but still I feel like I've not told him for his sake too. Should I tell him now?"

"Why are you asking me, Dutty? This is, I don't know, maybe this is between you and him. If you think you're right, it's your decision. I don't think the boy needs to know."

"What about when he's older, Horgan, what about then?"

"Maybe later. But I don't know that he'll find out. He believes you."

"He'll find out."

"He won't reproach you, Dutty."

"You wouldn't tell him now, then?"

"Maybe not while he's still a boy, still got a boy's spirit."

"That makes me feel better, Horgan. My conscience has been bothering me lately."

"He won't reproach you."

"I hope your daddy ..."

Horgan interrupts him, "I don't think he'll get better, do you?"

"Well." And then Dutton lets go of the eggs he's been holding.

"I'm sorry, Dutty."

"You know, Horgan, you were always your daddy's little boy."

"Still am," Horgan says, pushing himself up from the table. "Anything else, Dutty?"

"No, I guess. I'll go see your daddy this morning. See you at the game too."

"Well, keep them kids off the phone."

"I will, Horgan. Sure you don't want this egg?"

"Well, yeah, give it here." And the old man passes it to him, hand to hand, and Horgan slips it in his coat pocket.

"You sure you want to leave now?"

Horgan again feels something slipping. "You want to go fishing or something?"

"No, Horgan, no."

"Well, I guess I better be getting back to the station then." The old man nods down at him. He fills up the hole of the doorway. "See ya," Horgan says, and turns off the porch and heads for the fire truck. Pillsneck comes from around the corner of the house then, and clamps himself to Horgan's thigh and calf like a horny terrier.

"Wait, Coach, wait," he pants, holding tightly as Horgan lurches across the barnyard, taking a good step with his left leg and then dragging the right up after it, the one with the boy attached.

"Get off my leg, Pillsneck," Horgan says, "I've got to go to work."

"Coach, c'mon, c'mon, Coach. Let's win this one, Coach!"

Shrugsby stands on the porch with his grandpa, screaming "Pork sword!" again and again.

"Why aren't you sliding into chickens, Pillsneck?" Horgan asks, latching onto a grab bar on the truck and pulling. He shakes his leg as if he's trying to get the cuff straight.

"Let me pitch, Coach. For God's sake, let me pitch!" Pillsneck lets go of Horgan's thigh so he can get a better grip on his belt. Horgan takes hold of the grab bar firmly, throws his helmet and coat up on the seat of the truck, sees the axe but thinks better of it, thinks about it again when the boy bites him on the one piece of flab he owns, above his hip bone, and finally decides on taking a handful of Pillsneck's hair and slamming his head up against the running board when the old man and Shrugsby arrive and pry Pillsneck loose, holding him in the dirt while Horgan climbs aboard, grinds the gears, and roars off.

On the dirt road of red dust, away from the farm, he has to consciously make himself slow down. The wind is blowing in his face and his foot jams the 2×4 block hard to the floor. He cannot figure out why he was in such a hurry with Pillsneck, and even with the old man. Things were getting dangerous. Even if his father only had what time there was left for him, a week, a month, he himself had all day long, the whole rest of his life. He had to remember that.

- 4 -

What he knew of the old man, his father's old best
man, Dutton: that he had been his father's best man,
not only at the wedding, but since then too, since
Horgan was born and his mother left; since and
before, before the wedding, growing up together and
at college, where they'd roomed together forty-two
or -three years ago, and where Horgan's dad had met
his mom. Dutton and his father shared a dorm room
together but they weren't in school. The room was
part of their salary as groundskeepers. They shared
the room for almost ten years, single and unattached,
walking and working among the comings and goings
of the students, winking at each other, looking out at
the rears of girls from underneath the brims of their
caps, pulling up weeds. Then, after the almost ten
years, when they were both thirty, they both married. They had to give up the room. Both men kept
their groundskeeper jobs for a few more months, till
Horgan's mom left. Then Horgan's dad, carrying
Horgan, followed Dutton and his wife to Eckley.
Dutton bought a farm and came into town once a
week with his wife and son to have dinner with
Horgan and his dad. Horgan's father started a nursery, did odd jobs, and was elected Eckley's mayor.
He was mayor, on and off, for almost twenty years.

Dutton, Horgan thought, was the next best man to his father he'd ever met. He was big, and he had a way of bringing people in under his big arms with his big voice, and Horgan had never worried about him the way he'd worried over his father. He had been a little sad for him a couple times, when he lost his boy and daughter-in-law to the car wreck, and when he lost his wife, who'd stayed for thirty-eight years. But being sad for someone was not the same as being worried for them. Dutton's son had given him a grandson before he died, left him in his stead, and Dutton's wife had stayed. He'd had the extra thirty-seven years.

- 5 -

By mid-morning the sky is galvanized too and the mourning of the tin in earnest has begun. Water-grey, blue, silver-mottled, the air picks up tin tones and looks like it will never rust. And the wind moves through this, bleary-eyed, tearstained, and makes the barns hum, the background sound of all the life that goes on here. The wind rolls a gate and warps it slowly on its bleak hinges, and it wails. It's heard for miles, the wailing and yawing against the mourning tin, the country wearing on itself, chafing and sand-blasting, removing the vertical, singing to level, do-ing it with blueness and religion, dryly.

Watching time, that's what this country's like, Horgan thinks, and he slides his chair back against the big tin door of the firehouse, back in the shade, and then he wheels with the gathering birds around Miss Eckley's elevator, spiraling downward. He sud-denly feels used, like the hour that happens twice when he sets the clock back to Standard Time. He'd called Kidder to apologize for the spilled oatmeal, to tell her about the false alarm. He'd rushed to the door to find it was only the wind, a branch knocking against the side of his skull.

He had a good mind to take his fire truck and go looking for cats. It was their affected self-assurance that aggravated him, their impassioned conviction. Run a fire truck up on one of them, sirens screaming, and see how completely he falls apart. Hmmph. It is good to hate one thing, up front and without reservation, Horgan thinks. You can turn to it at a time like this. And if that one thing does not deserve the least notion of animosity, if it is a stuffed animal, a terry cloth towel, a bunny, a saintly virtue, so much the better. The recuperative benefits of hating it are quadrupled. For Horgan it is the cat. He leans back in his chair, bangs his head on the tin, and lets himself fall sweetly into his abomination. He'd seen a cat dead on the road the week before; that was something; but an instantaneous death probably too good for it. There was the time he saw two Dobermans chasing a cat around the corner of a building: that was sport. And once, over the radio—it was a long time ago and perhaps it wasn't true—he'd heard of a cat ban. A complete ban, not just your scattered and infrequent cat lynchings and drownings, but a planet-wide defelination. Cat blood flowing on the pavement. That would be sport. But the ecstasy of this thought, the computations and graphics of the possibility, becomes at last too much for him, and he lapses back into the concrete serenity of his memory.

It had happened just three days ago, when he'd gone to Miss Eckley's to ask for a donation.

The Eckley Little League team was hoping to get T-shirts for the big game. Since the shirts would have her name on them, Horgan thought Miss Eckley would at least kick in ten bucks. He'd parked the fire truck out front and walked around the side of the house to the back door. The cats, dozens of them, coiled about his calves like a pair of pants just unsnapped, and he nearly tripped twice. They were everywhere, the cats, mewing and purring about with their air of indifferent independence. They slipped off of ledges, out of sheds, peered down from the roof, and crouched in the overgrown hedges and grass in the backyard. Their accumulated and broadcast toys squeaked under his foot. The back porch was a carnival toss of food and water bowls. Cat food filled and spilled from them, sickeningly cute shapes and colors, like thousands of jacks. Horgan was standing in front of the door, knocking, when he noticed a grey striped Tom lounging on a windowsill nearby. The Tom looked up at Horgan, surveyed him casually, licked his front paw in a gesture of complete disgust and turned his head away. And this is the sweet memory. Hearing no approaching footsteps from inside, he quickly snatched the Tom by the scruff of the neck, backed a few feet away from the house, and then tossed the cat lightly against the cracked wood siding to see if he would stick. And he did. The cat clutched the siding with all four sprung, clawed paws, held for an instant, then sprang off and away. This was sport. Horgan picked up another cat. The second cat stuck too, but banged his head in the process and sprang off and away rather woozily. This, this, was sport. With these successes in hand he backed away a few more feet, picked up a limp Tabby (and at this distance he would probably have to throw the cat overhand), raised it to shoulder level, and Miss Eckley opened the back door.

Across the Route, under the halo of birds in descent, Miss Eckley knocks about the tin walls of her office. She rages at the pflop of bird droppings on her roof. The dust of her operation begins to filter in under the door when she moves back behind her metal desk, beneath the three engravings on the wall, and picks up the phone. "Akton," she says, "go now and pick up Double-nought and tell him he can burn that old shack on my place." Then she pauses, listening, her eyes blankly staring up at the engravings: one of the Victorian mansion her father built, a great many doors and windows facing the street; one of the elevator in its prime; and between these two a print of Donner Pass. "You do what I say," she says, as if to a child. "And when it gets going, call the Fire Department. I don't want anything else burning out there, but I want Horgan occupied." And she hangs up, sits down for a moment, then rises, pushing the chair back into the tin wall behind her.

"Oochie, goochie, goochie goo," Kidder says, rubbing her flat belly and giggling to herself in the Baby Needs aisle of the Eckley Supermarket. She wears a pair of jeans and one of Horgan's old blue work shirts, the tail flapping loosely about her knees. Her hair is pinned in a flagrant bun. She pushes her cart, giggling, hopping on and off occasionally, opening and closing the baby seat, testing the aisle out, another trial run; pushes her cart past the diapers, the boxes of six to thirteen pounders, the twelve to twenty-four pounders, and the nineteen to thirty-five pounders. Goes back to the six to thirteen pounders and puts a box in her cart. She lingers, stalls, back down the aisle toward the checkout lanes, examining a box of Q-tips, a pair of vinyl pants, a trainer cup, lingering, pushing her cart, running her hand over a bib. The pacifier doesn't seem to bother her, nor the Similac, nor the countless varieties of vitamin-C-added, strained and creamed food. It's at the end of the aisle where she picks up a soft-bite spoon. She spins, wheels back down the aisle, and reshelves the box of diapers.

At the checkout counter Kidder's classmate, the second runner-up homecoming queen candidate, rings up her purchases. The second runner-up speaks, and as she speaks she sticks her tongue out of her mouth, between her teeth, between every two words.

"Same old thing, Kidder?" she asks.

Kidder wipes her face, smiling. "Yeah. But I go to the doctor this afternoon. Maybe then."

"I can always tell it when you come out of that aisle, honey. You can tell me all about it at the game. My little Yanks is already out there somewhere practicing. How's Horgan?"

"He's okay. Had a false alarm this morning. Got back and called me and I thought he was gonna cry for it. Sometimes I think about setting fire to our house to satisfy him."

"Poor thing." There are scars there on the tip of her tongue.

"Well, I picked up some SpaghettiOs for his lunch. That ought to perk him up. He deserves it after all the vitamins and wheat germ I've poked down him," Kidder says, and points out her car to the box boy.

"Well, Kidder, honey, maybe you ought to have him go have a talk with my Burt. You know, man-to-man. Other than that, I'd give you one of my kids if I could."

Kidder pauses, slowly replacing her checkbook, and then comes up brightly. "Thanks. I'll try to get Horgan over there sometime for some advice. Say," she asks, "say, can you remember that thing we used to scream when we were in school? Every time we'd see a baby carriage? I've been trying to come up with it all morning. Starts with Blubber, dubber... something..."

And the second runner-up spits into it, a trivia contest winner, "Rubber baby buggy brghmp..." and a fine jet of blood sprays onto the stainless steel countertop, then dribbles between the fingers she clamps over her mouth.

"Thanks, honey," Kidder says, picking up a peck of paper sacks and flinging them into the air as she leaves.

Old man Dutton drops the two boys off in front of the supermarket, honks at Kidder as she crosses in front of him, and then drives off toward the hospital. The two boys walk inside.

"I gotta get Coach's attention," Pillsneck says, stalking the aisles.

"I gotta get some gum," Shrugsby answers. "Meet you at the counter." Shrugsby picks up eleven packages of baseball cards and a dozen pieces of gum besides, because the gum that comes with the cards is made of plywood. He throws them up on the checkout counter and says, "Hey, lady, your tongue's bleedin'." A chicken feather wafts from his hair to the floor.

"Don't you call me lady, little Shrugsby. You know my name. You seen my little Yanks today? Left the house with his glove and bat at 6:30 this morning and I got neighbors with dents in their cars."

"No, ma'am, I haven't seen him."

"He's only nine years old," she says, dabbing her tongue with a Kleenex.

"I'm only eight, ma'am."

"Well, you see him, tell him I'm going to whip his butt when I get to the ball game this evening."

"Yes, ma'am," Shrugsby says, "I'll tell him you'll

whip his butt." Pillsneck walks up behind and throws a box of kitchen matches on the stainless steel.

"Thirty-two cents, Pillsneck. You pitched a pretty game last week," Yanks' mom says.

"Yes, ma'am. My daddy said to put these on his ticket."

"Okay. You two be good. Bye bye." And the two boys walk out under the galvanized sky.

When the automatic doors shut behind them, Shrugsby gets behind Pillsneck and tries to put him in a headlock. "Gimme them matches," he says. But Pillsneck breaks loose, scattering the cards and gum, and he is off and around the corner before Shrugsby can gather half of his broadcast supply for the game. He stands there, two-gum-fisted, and says, over and over, "Oh, my God, oh, my God, he's out there somewhere with them matches."

"What are you doing with that cat?" Miss Eckley said.

Horgan held the cat in the air just above his head. He glanced up at it, thought, well, hell, and said, "This cat here has fleas on its belly, Miss Eckley. You ought to bring all these cats (and once again a deep sense of nausea had overcome him for the thing he was about to say in spite of himself) down to the firehouse weekend after next. I'm having a free pet dip."

"Put that cat down."

He tried to set the limp animal gently on the earth. But its own legs refused to support it. It kept falling over. Then he tried to pick the cat up again to set it straight but it was like trying to pick up a wet noodle on a countertop. He thought he might pinch it in half. God, it was a disgusting animal. He had a great sense of guilt when he raised back up to look at Miss Eckley. He somehow felt that she was going to accuse him of breaking all of the cat's legs.

"Miss Eckley," he said, putting his thumbs in his front pockets, "I'm collecting donations for the Little League. We'd like to get the boys T-shirts for the game this Saturday. The back of them will say 'Eckley Little League.' I was wondering if you might want to contribute."

She stood up on the porch, her arms crossed over her bosom. He knew she wouldn't invite him into the house; no one had been in there but Miss Eckley since her father died forty years ago. Her reclusiveness and her refusal to even let a plumber in the house (one had come once and she'd brought the broken fittings out to him on the back porch where he did what he could, instructed as best he could, and she took his tools back in the house to fix the pipes herself) caused a great many rumors, but none of them founded on anything substantial as far as Horgan knew. The rumors: that she kept a dead man inside; that the house was full of her hoarded cash; that a distant marriage had failed in the making and that a huge moldering cake sat upstairs, rot and insect infested, spider webs broaching the still air; that she wasn't actually a "Miss" at all, had actually said "I do" to a man in a weak and distracted moment, then had realized her mistake and come home to hide from him. Horgan thought of the stories as he stood there. Maybe he could run by her and get a peek inside. Yet she stood there, small but firm, familiar but mean, a chip of something dried hard on the hearth.

"I understand you're a drinker," she said.

"What?" Horgan said. He hadn't expected that line, how could he, but he should have somehow guessed it. She leaped to the personal; she took every advantage.

"I understand that you drink liquor at the ball games."

"A beer, Miss Eckley, or two, but what's that got to do with…"

"I think you should stop that."

He just had a beer or two during the fourth inning stretch. It was usually roaring hot in the evening out on Eckley Field.

"Well, Miss Eckley…"

"It's a bad influence on them boys."

"Well, Miss Eckley…"

She interrupted again. He was beginning to get a little pissed. She said, "I'll buy all the shirts when you cut that out. That's my final word on it. Well?"

Horgan put his tongue between his molars and bit down hard because it was less conspicuous than sitting down and pounding his own nuts with his fist. If she hadn't said it with such authority, as if she had a right to tell him what to do, he might have succumbed. Because she was probably right. He probably oughtn't to drink beers during the game. So he clenched the idea of blackmail, and said, "Miss Eckley, what I do isn't any of your concern. I came asking for the boys."

And she said, "Fine, those boys aren't my responsibility," and turned back into the house, closed the door on his face. He kicked a rubber mouse with a bell in it across the yard. It beleagured him to no end to watch four cats have the time of their lives chasing it. That was another reason he hated cats.

They ate mice. And birds. He saw now why Miss Eckley liked them.

Suddenly above him, something is thundering. He comes out of his cat reverie, drops the chair back to level, and looks up into the bright day sun. A street of tin on the firehouse roof is flapping against the rafters. The constant wind has torn it loose.

Ooper and Akton, the county deputy sheriff, stomp through the dry weeds in the vacant lot next to Miss Eckley's house, back to an old double garage that's about to fall in upon itself. Ooper is almost foaming with the prospect. He has the mouth and lips of a human but behind the tautness he's dogtoothed in a sea of saliva; his fangy, anxious smile unnerves Akton.

Ooper says, "You just stand back and watch the hand of God."

"You be careful, you crazy bastard. Why Miss Eckley fools with you I'll never know." Akton backs up a little as he says this.

Ooper turns, the gasoline can in one hand and the matches in the other, and takes a step toward him. "Because she understands," he says, and for a moment it almost looks as if he will sit down on the can and light matches, the way someone else might pare their nails, as he explains, "It's all in print, has been for years, what's going to happen and how, and it pleases me to be a part of His handiwork. I see now that it pleases Miss Eckley too. I've been after her to let me burn this old shack for two years now."

"Well," and Akton backs up some more, "this wind's awful high. You be careful. I'm going to go get Horgan."

"You ought to stay and watch," Ooper pleads, yelling after Akton. "Won't be no good just me watching it. I already understand. This fire, small as it will be, is a lesson as well as His will.''

"You go ahead," Akton yells back at him from behind the cruiser and then he jumps in and locks the door, settles back as best he can to watch the fire get going.

Along with the wind the heat rises, in blurred layers, from the earth and tin. The Route and the elevator shimmer, vibrate almost in the blasted air, and a bird lights in Horgan's shadow.

The six ball-playing sons of the five fathers begin to gather, like birds, at the Dairy Mart. They come walking from all over town, gloves in hand, tossing balls up into the sky and moving under their fall. Sickopoose and Witherspoon are brought in from the country by their mothers. The boys hover about in ones and twos, smacking their mitts, sucking on cool pops. When Yanks shows up, his arrival coming two minutes after his ball's and the crack of his bat, they form a V pattern, Witherspoon in the lead, his catcher's mask pulled down over his stubborn mug. "Hey, batter, batter, batter, batter," they mumble, then chant, for the sheer intimidation of it, building up their collective courage. Their calls, batter, batter, batter, rise slowly, like the rising of music in a darkened theatre.

He writes, feebly, with a great deal of sketching effort, his wishes on 5×7 note cards because Dutton hasn't learned sign language yet. There is a tube placed down his throat this morning and the nurses have him propped up on the bed.

Old Dutton says, after taking the card in his big hand and reading it, "Don't just keep writing 'no' on this card, Joe. I want you to give me leave to tell him. I want to tell him now."

Horgan's father is a great shrunken sink hole in the earth. The land is smooth and level around him for miles but he is fallen in for lack of moisture. His temples, cheeks, the sockets of his eyes and the hollow of his throat look like someone has put their thumb there heavily.

He writes "no" on the card again.

"You give me leave, mister. If you won't do it, give me leave. I want to tell him now so he can see you afterwards. I don't want to be left with this after you've gone. I talked to him this morning already and worked all around it. I was going to tell him then, but I didn't. But I'm here now asking you."

"Telling me," he writes on the card.

"Have it your way then. Telling you. But give me your consent. I don't want to be left with it after you're gone and there is just me to live with it. He wouldn't understand then. He might even call me a liar."

"She'll come back," he writes.

"She hasn't, and she won't never. Years and years it's been," Dutton says, sitting on the edge of the chair near the bed, his arms and hands hanging from his body into his lap. "Time for you to see that and think about Horgan."

Tears well up in Horgan's father's eyes and he writes, trembling, on the big card, "not fair."

Dutton stands up to see water upon his face. It is incongruous, water upon the so long dry face. "I'm sorry," Dutton says and he sits back down and rubs the dying man's arm. "When did you get worse, Joe? Last night?"

"Last night," he writes.

"Much worse?"

"Little," he writes. "Tired," he writes. "Yes, Horgan," he writes.

"Okay," Dutton says, "good man," patting the back of Horgan's father's hand. "I'll sit here and have lunch with you now, tell you all what's happened to me since yesterday. Then I'll go find Horgan."

- 6 -

Horgan climbs down from the tin roof and says,
"Boy, it's hot," then says it again, "Boy, it's hot,"
and thinks, after the second saying, that every time
he comes outside, or finishes any little project, he
says, "Boy, it's hot." I never say, he thinks, "Boy,
it's flat," even though it is just as flat as it is hot,
flatter maybe. He thinks he says the word "really"
and the phrase "everybody and their dog" too often
too, as if he questioned every statement made by
man, and that everyone indeed had a dog to take
along with them. He didn't even have a dog.

He takes the hammer, ladder, and sack of leadhead nails back into the firehouse. If the roof was a
griddle the firehouse was a cheap oven. So he goes
back outside and says, "Boy, it's hot," realizes it
and adds aloud, "REALLY? EVERYBODY AND
THEIR DOG! YOU IDIOT!" He sits in the thinner
slice of shade. Even though he leans back in the chair
his boots still get sunlight on them. He feels the Tater
Tots of his toes begin to boil in their own sweat. He
looks at his browned hands and forearms and realizes he is being slowly cooked.

The whole country is a skillet, and he remembers, as
a boy, jumping up and down on the sidewalks and
streets of Eckley in his bare feet cherishing the few

brief moments of flight, when his feet did not fry. At the lean age of six he could understand the complex reasoning behind a *changement* move in ballet. "They grew up in a flat, hot country," he told his father, watching the traveling ballet company that had stopped for a bite at the Dairy Mart when he was a boy.

He lifted his boots and did a quick *changement* in the hot morning air. Then he looked around to see if anybody might have noticed. He was always doing that—acting before calculating the possibility of personal embarrassment on a nuclear scale. It seemed a man ought to improve some from the age of six to forty. He had done that same thing at the Dairy Mart, lifted his sneakered feet under the table and done a *changement* some thirty-four years ago, and the dance company had claimed him on the spot, offered to take him along on the road as a mascot. He was the tomato on his hamburger by the time he got out of there. Maybe he should have gone.

That, he thinks, and he raises his hand with pointed finger and shakes it, that was the first blatant sign of his bleak destiny. If it weren't for Kidder.

Sometimes he felt like a bug banging his life out on a window pane. It was so hard to look beyond his own reflection to see the world.

But that was it. There it was.

He stares blankly across the Route at the elevator, bringing his knees up to his chest and folding his arms around them.

He hadn't taken the ballet company opportunity: faint augury, true, but explicit enough in retrospect. He had thought at one time, two or three years after he became a fireman, that he might put a sign up over the firehouse door with a sort of personal motto: "They also serve who only stand and wait." He'd been in the service only because they'd come after him; he'd joined the railroad in the same manner that he'd joined high school or the service—it was there and you were expected to go if you didn't work at the elevator; the fireman job was a pure gift from Dinks; and finally, it was Kidder who had pursued him. He'd never had the courage to take the responsibility for his own life, much less someone else's.

In the Air Force he'd been a boom operator on a KC-135 for most of his eight-year hitch. If he'd known how dangerous the position was when it was offered he'd have turned it down too. It was all too easy to knock a fighter plane out of the sky.

Horgan, thinking, lets the chair fall back down on all four legs and bends over, staring at the red earth between his boots.

He would lie flat on his stomach in the very tail end of the 135, an in-flight fuel tanker, and fly the boom with its small "ruddervator" wings. His airplane would reach its destination and then circle in the vast, open sky, waiting for the small jets. They would come slowly, one at a time, like minnows, up to the rear of the plane and Horgan would fly the boom, with its attached fuel line, into the small port on the nose of the jets and refuel them. He controlled a midair umbilical. Before each refueling he always had to think about running the boom through the fighter's cockpit, and into the pilot's chest, just so he wouldn't do that. He never had. And the Strategic Air Command, always belligerent about their preparedness, practiced him and his airplane over the Arctic and the equator, day and night, during some of the worst storms they could find. The boom sometimes seemed to bounce off clouds and shred before his eyes before he coaxed it and the fighter pilot together. He flew a few missions over Vietnam, but was never in any more danger than his own refueling operation put him in. Most of these flights were for refueling bombers on their way to or from a sortie over the combat area. The big eight-engined B-52s would come up from behind and under, to within kicking distance, Horgan thought (the boom, fully extended, was only forty feet long). And Horgan would perform his phallic entry three or four feet in front of the plane's cockpit. It was almost as embarrassing as it was dangerous. He used to smile down at the pilot and co-pilot when he was finished, drawing out, the last few drops of fuel falling on their windshield.

But the work, the refueling, took up only a small portion of the actual flight time. There was mainly the climb, the wait, and the descent. And he, lying face down in the rear of the plane, would watch not where he was going, but only where he had been. He constantly had the sense of leaving, that everything he saw was in the past. The only time he ever knew where he was going was when they flew in circles, waiting, around and around, over the same piece of earth. The fighters and bombers, an occasional transport, would fly up to him, refuel, and bank away, leave him lying there. He would watch their silvery or camouflaged descent, descent in a definite direction, as long as he could, and then would turn back to the place where he had been.

During his sixth year the Air Force offered to send him to officer's school, a distinction he turned down. It had just scared him, that's all. And when his second tour was up he didn't re-enlist because the idea of officer's school made him so nervous. He couldn't accept the idea of command. As it was they were giving him stripes at the rate of one a year, in a sense nudging him into responsibility. He wouldn't have it. He got out.

"Well, I got out, that's all," Horgan says aloud and stands up. He looks up into the stark sun and thinks, I've got that inspection at eleven. It is almost ten now. He carries his chair back inside the firehouse. He walks to a corner of the tin building over the smooth concrete floor and lays hold of the broom. He hopes, as he turns, that he will have something to do, that the wind has blown a bit of dried grass or some sand in the big door and onto the floor. He finishes turning, bends down and puts his eye as close to the floor as his cheek and nose will let him, and sees sand and dust everywhere, a perfect Sahara on his firehouse floor. So he sweeps. He makes eight or ten good long shoves with the three-foot broom and realizes he is already done. He puts the broom back in its corner. He gives the fire engine a once over with a dust rag, finds a screw a quarter-turn loose, so he takes out the toolbox and checks every screw and bolt on the truck. That done, he walks back to his desk inside and makes sure the calendar page doesn't need to be flipped. Then he puts his chair back outside. ("Boy, it's hot.") Just another hour, he thinks, and I'll have that inspection to do. He leans back against the tin again and now the shade just barely takes in his eyes. The cars of the Burlington-Northern clash, and clank forward a few feet in front of the elevator. The birds rise for a squawking moment then resettle.

And after that first little false start after coming home from the Air Force, he connected with the

Burlington-Northern because they had a deal for veterans. He rode the caboose on a grain and livestock line for six years, watching again the place where he had just been, the long converging tracks behind him. Such a feeling of being dragged, he thought. And then the line said he had enough time in to apply for an engineer position, and after that everyone on the line and in every yard was asking him if he'd applied yet so he'd gotten out of that too.

Hey, wait a minute, weren't cats dangerous to pregnant women?

He'd gotten out of them. Pushing himself forward with his own hand was an awkward operation anyway. He had to labor his wrist and nearly break an elbow.

He looks down the Route to the wavering "La Motel" sign and wishes they'd take the "Shark Free Pool" note off of it. It embarrassed the whole town.

The only conscious decision he'd made concerning his career was quitting the job at the elevator after his fourth day there. Miss Eckley seemed to expect miracles from him, worked him harder than anyone else. It was just after he'd gotten out of the Air Force that he took her job offer and subsequently quit. He'd had eight years of being bossed around in the service; he hadn't been looking for more of it at home. But it wasn't just her constant vigilance and pressure on the job that made him quit. They'd had that argument over the birds. On the morning of the fourth day he'd come to work early, like she'd told him to, and he'd caught her feeding the birds. He thought she was feeding the birds. But it was an action so far removed from his conception of her that he moved in closer and saw the tiny white pellets of poison. Before he could say a word she lifted the sack toward him and said, "Help me with this."

"I won't do it," he said.

"These birds spread disease, congregated as they are." She was a younger woman then, forty-six or -seven, and Horgan couldn't let himself hate her as much then.

He said, "Never been any disease around here."

"Because I've been controlling it for twenty-five years."

Horgan then understood the bodies of birds he'd occasionally found in his backyard as he grew up. They'd eaten the poison, and feeling it, had tried to fly away from the sickness. He remembered something else then, something more recent, something he'd heard but paid no particular attention to as he walked out to Miss Eckley in the field bordering the elevator. He looked down at his feet and the ground around them. There on the ground, fine as the blades of grass and intermixed, were the white bleached and brittle bones and skulls of birds. They crunched beneath his step. Then he did not need her to be old and ugly to hate her.

He said, "Somehow this isn't right," and he turned and left. She didn't call after him.

It seems, Horgan thinks, moving his chair back just inside the big doorway and sitting down, that life is like morning and dusk all day long, just when you think things are about to change. He had waited to be sixteen, then twenty-one, then thirty, and now he is forty, and he still feels like he hasn't hit sixteen yet. Nothing like killing time. Perhaps if he'd collected sock and tie hangers he might have something to talk about.

Horgan makes a funny face in three directions and goes back to the office for his Fire Prevention Code handbook. Even though he has inspected the elevator thirteen times over the last seven years he still likes to go by the book. It seems to intimidate the old lady just enough, the book does, to let him get through the inspection without her beating him with a piece of steel. He sits back down and thumbs through it, occasionally pausing to wipe the sweat from his eyebrows. Overloaded circuits, electrical cords subject to foot traffic, improper trash receptacles, flammable or combustible liquids stored improperly, adequate fire extinguishers, etc. Run-of-the-mill requirements. He mostly checked to see if Miss Eckley was providing adequate ventilation for the dust she worked up. Dust, any kind of dust, mixed with air in the proper proportion becomes explosive and can be ignited by a spark or flame. There really wasn't much he could do at the elevator. There wasn't anything to burn; it was built of sheet iron, steel, and concrete. There was only the dust to explode. It would explode and that would be it. No fire of any consequence would follow. His only job after an explosion might be to go in after the dead men, but the county rescue squad would probably handle that now.

He throws the book up in the seat of the fire truck, climbs up himself, and sits in front of the big wheel. Not long now, he thinks. God, it's a great feeling, sitting up here. And he thinks again about his false alarm of the morning, and grimaces for Pillsneck clinging to his leg. Maybe he ought to pitch him. If it would make a difference he might, but there would be no beating that Springtown team, even if he had his own father, in his prime, pitching for him. Besides, there was something about the way Pillsneck flung himself at you. He'd let Gaspar have his turn. They'd lose by a few more runs but losing is losing. There isn't any use trying to get around that.

A FLATLAND FABLE

He looks out of the firehouse and up into the faultless sky and thinks, it'll never rain. He oozes back down into the seat, running his hands over the big steering wheel. Maybe I can put one of them doorknobs on this thing and really turn a corner.

"Your father in his prime," he has heard Dutton say, if once, a million times, starting the old proud story. "Your father in his prime, he was almost as big as me. Had bigger hands. But tall and lanky and looser than me. My God, how he could throw a fastball, and hit anybody else's half a mile. He'd wrap his lanky fingers around a baseball about four times and fling it and you'd think he never really threw a baseball at all, but the idea of a baseball, and it never even dimly dawned on you that you could hit that idea with a piece of wood you held in your hands. That was the very farthest thing from your mind. And the baseball scouts came to hold his hand in theirs and feel his grip; but he was only seventeen. They wrote up contract after contract and he signed them all but he was only seventeen and just barely that, so to make it legal his mother had to sign it too. And I was there too when he took it in to her, he was so proud, and I was there, and she said no. She said it again and again to each contract, saying no because she wouldn't have her son playing ball on Sunday. That's what the pro teams did then, played every Saturday and Sunday. So he didn't go. And when he turned twenty-one and didn't need her signature anymore on the contract he still didn't go because he needed her approval and she still wouldn't give that so he never went. And he and I got jobs as groundskeepers at the college then. We were in the city and it was easier for him not to think about baseball there. And when she died seven years later he still had the arm and fingers and they still wanted him but he said to me he was happy as a groundskeeper, and I could understand that, I was happy as a groundskeeper too, but I couldn't throw a fastball like that. So I think it was still his mother. He didn't go. I think it always tore me up more than him. I just know he would've been the best. But he was devoted.''

Horgan would hear the story from Dutty and understand why he had grown up with a baseball. Grew up with it, but never grew around it. He didn't get his father's height or his grip or his grace with a bat. He'd gotten his abilities from Doris before she left.

The trouble with his father was he trusted the wrong women: his mother, then Doris. His mother had ruined his career with her faith and Doris had left a month after Horgan was born. Horgan's father was still convinced she'd someday come back. It would almost be embarrassing if it wasn't so sad.

Kidder drives past, honking and holding a can of SpaghettiOs out of the car window and waving it. Horgan waves back. That was a can of SpaghettiOs, he thinks. Of course, now, with his waiting, there are only the hollow places of his face. Horgan almost feels guilty for having Kidder. But his father seems to love her as much as he does. Here, for his father, is someone else to trust, no questions asked. But Kidder, finally, is one worthy of it. His father wouldn't look at it that way, though. He thought all were worthy.

Even in his own life he could not explain the occurrence of Kidder. There is something that's happened. And he thinks of the two women he'd been with before her, the one who tasted like a nine-volt

battery, and the other, who was like sucking on his
Teddy Bear's plastic nose. And then Kidder, who
was like all the things that hadn't happened to him,
who was like possibility itself somehow. He met her
on the job. She worked at a kindergarten where
Horgan was giving a fire program for the kids. Telling them to crawl along the floor and not to open hot
doors. Kidder followed him right out the door when
he left and asked if he wasn't the one on the fire truck
five years before when she was third runner-up.

Horgan wanted to lie but said "yes" instead.

"I went to college," she said, "It took me five
years, but I'm back here for good as far as I know."

"I thought about you," Horgan said, looking for
humiliation, for something, anything.

Kidder said, "I've got to go to the grocery store
after work. You want to go?"

And he said, "Sure," thinking of the fourteen
years, thinking of her outrageous beauty.

And they had gone to the grocery store together
for the next year, seeing what each other liked. Then
they got married and went to the grocery store together when they could for another two years and
now they are trying to have a baby. I love you, he
thinks. I've always wanted someone like you to love,
and he lays on the horn for a good long forlorn blast.
The thing is that nothing is happening. He is as dry
as this drought. Kidder, what she says: things happen to you when you least expect them; a watched
clock doesn't tick; how a creek always looks the
same but really it's always moving, constantly different water under the bridge.

He looks up, still leaning on the steering wheel,
and sees that there is still forty-five minutes before

he has anything to do. He looks back away from the clock. I have waited and I have waited too long, he thinks. I am old, too, he thinks. Life is like morning and dusk, just when you think things are about to change, but it is that way all day long, all life long.

- 7 -

And he is still there on the fire engine, hanging precariously from the cab toward the big sideview mirror, his head flung back sharply, his eyes slotted down the line of his nose at the wide angle convex, trying to gauge the full bore of his own nostrils, when it all starts.

He hears the siren approach, doubts it, then believes again, and his heart begins to pound as he watches Akton skid to a halt in front of the firehouse door. He jumps from the cab and runs for the patrol car, toward Akton's screaming and beckoning, thinking, my father, my father, and he is almost crying with his fear and wonder when Akton's voice breaks through the power of his own beckoning arm and hand and Horgan hears him yelling, "Bring your fire truck, bring your fire truck," and he thinks, oh, oh, and almost collapses with his relief and his shame as he turns back toward the engine, putting his hand down on the red dirt to help the one buckled knee as he turns, thinking, fire, fire, thinking, this wind, this wind, and before he jumps back up into the cab he slams with the heel of his palm the big red button on the central support beam of the firehouse and Eckley is warned. The big fire siren rises on the wind over the town like a huge pterodactyl.

And he knows, following Akton, when he is within a block of whatever it is that's burning—not because he can see the smoke—the wind is blowing so hard that the smoke doesn't even have a chance to rise before it's swept away—or because he can smell it—he is upwind—but because he notices the scattered dozens of bicycles lying on their sides, on the sidewalks and in the street, like broken insects, the bikes the kids threw down when they heard of the fire. So he throttles down and screeches to a halt, not noticing where he stops, but stopping because that's what Akton did and he is following him. He looks up, and he is parked in front of Miss Eckley's. And the shack in her vacant lot, and her vacant lot, and one whole end of her house are on fire.

Her house, a bone on the plains, the biggest house in Eckley, that her father built when she was just a child. It burns up the height of the wall next to the vacant lot, and flames blow out of the upper and lower floor windows like curtains on that end, and smoke seeps from the seams of the copper roof. The smoke is black and blue and grey and white and streams along the roof and ground, and Horgan watches the orange sparks stream with it.

By the time he is out of the cab and down on the sidewalk with Akton, Ooper is there too, running up from the far side of the house, his eyes tearing with the smoke, but before he can say a word Akton draws his nightstick, and, swinging abruptly, horizontally, strikes him hard across the ear and cheekbone. Ooper falls back on the ground and rolls, covering his head, and Horgan finds himself not following Akton but heading him off, tackling him at the knees before he can hit Ooper again. He throws him to the ground, scales up Akton's body to get a hand on the nightstick which he still holds. And doing that, screams into Akton's ear, "Have you checked inside? Is there anybody inside?" and Akton stops struggling.

"No, no, I haven't. Ain't nobody in there, goddammit. Get off of me."

"I'll check," Horgan says, still holding the hand of the nightstick, and as he gets up he yells, "When the volunteers get here, tell them to watch for fires downwind." And he gets up, putting his foot on the nightstick as long as he can to get away clearly. As he does Akton lets go of the stick and Horgan watches the anger leave his face, turn to something else.

The deputy gets up and yells, yelling now over the noise of the fire, "They might not come."

"What?" Horgan yells, backing up toward the burning house.

"She might not let them."

"Who won't?"

"Miss Eckley."

"What?" he says, "You go get them," he orders, and he turns to run to the back of the house because the front door and most of the windows in front are boarded up.

He turns and takes a step or two but Akton has him by the shoulder. "I tried to put it out," he pleads. "I tried to, but when I picked up the water hose in back it just crumbled in my hands. It was all coiled up but it just crumbled it was so dry. No water would come out of that spicket either, back there or out front here."

"Akton, go get those men." Horgan turns again, running, rounds the corner of the house and leaps up the back stairs, finds the door unlocked and opens it into darkness and light smoke. He steps inside, and stepping on a cat, slips. He slips, his head banging on the threshold. Ooper helps him up.

Ooper holds onto his hand and says, "This is our Father's fire."

And although Horgan knew that God lived in his town, he also understood that other than this knowledge, all else is left up to him. He says, "Okay, John, you go back out to the street now," and he pushes him back out the doorway gently.

As they spoke two more cats squeezed out of the door between their legs. Horgan steps back in, rubbing his head, and lets his eyes become accustomed to the darkness. The first thing he notices are the pairs of eyes looking back at him. Cats in the darkness, everywhere, under furniture, up on cabinets, crouched along the walls. He yells, "Anybody in here?" twice, before he begins his search through the house. He trots from one room to the next, yelling, through the antique but impeccably kept rooms, looking for things that should be saved. But there is so much, the house is so crowded, and the smoke now so thick, that he turns from a burning room, from watching a wall of faded and curled newspaper clippings and framed diplomas burn, something familiar there, but in the turning he nearly falls over another cat. He catches himself with one hand before he hits the floor, finds himself face to face with the hissing cat, who reaches out with his paw and draws the sprung claws across Horgan's cheek. Horgan jumps back against a wall and kicks at the cat. It infuriates him. He cannot believe it, rubbing the blood off his face with his clinched fist. He runs back through the house, the smoke thick now and he coughing in it, to the back door. He runs, thinking, the thing about smoke is you can't breathe in it. He throws the door open, chocking it open with a gallon jug of water (and there are dozens of jugs there, stacked along the wall next to the door), and he yells, even louder than before, "Okay, come on!" but none of the cats come; then to his own chagrin and disbelief, he yells, "Here, kitty, kitty, kitty, here kitty, kitty, kitty," every grating syllable sliding over his teeth like sandpaper, and one cat bolts out, but the rest stay put, still able to breathe under the furniture. So he goes after them, after throwing open a few windows, since the house was lost anyway. The first, a grey Tom, scratches him on the palms of both hands before Horgan gets him out from underneath a bookcase and throws him out an open window with his neck taut hiss and cat scream. He goes from bookcase to sofa, sofa to loveseat, loveseat to chair, room to room, throwing cats out the windows. They draw as much blood as they can from his biceps and knuckles, across his ribs and chest, and down the length of his forearms. They scream as he grabs them by the scruff of the neck, by a back leg, by the head or tail, and they scream when he tosses them in long graceful arcs from the dark, smoky rooms to the bright summer day. The cats hiss at having their lives saved. They land in the grass and dirt and run up and down the street. The children of the fallen bicycles chase them. The children's dogs pass them. Horgan turns over the dry, dust-choked furniture till he finds no more cats, and then he himself runs from the thick smoke, the desiccated house, into the stunning breeze of the day, coughing.

He stumbles back to the front of the house, and finds just the truck there, still sitting there. Where are my volunteers, he thinks. My God, he thinks, I can't do this alone. From the crowd of onlookers—women, children, cats, and old men—young Whit spurts on his banana seat bicycle. He pedals heavily to Horgan's side, throws down his bike, another broken grasshopper, and says, "Coach, I saw the ashes come over my backyard. What do you want me to do?"

And Horgan says, "Right. Get back on your bike, get all these kids on their bikes, and go downwind looking for fires. They'll be everywhere. Come back and tell me where they are. Don't you fool with them, okay?"

"Okay, Coach," and Whit picks up his bike, baseball glove dangling from the handlebars, and pedals off.

The fire is huge now, flames spinning up out of the open windows, the smoke twirling beyond and then caught in the leveling wind. Women with running water hoses stand in their front yards all the way down the street.

Horgan runs back to the fire truck, yelling, "Everybody get back, everybody get back," and starts to push two old men out of the way when he realizes they are two of his volunteers, the only two that don't work at the elevator, the two ancient Witherspoons, great uncles to his catcher, come from their farm three miles out in the country. Their helmets are too big for them. Horgan can't help smiling when he thinks of turtles. He yells, "It's just us, boys. Help me with this hose."

"Yep," the one old man yells.

"Yep," the other old man yells.

And Horgan takes the big plug wrench and one end of the hose and starts down the street, dragging the hose as if it was a stubborn dog. He passes through a fence of women, passes a small crowd ringing Ooper, who stands a good two feet above them.

"Glorify ye the Lord in the fires," Ooper screams at the crowd, "for the Lord thy God is a consuming fire, and for by fire will the Lord plead with all flesh."

Horgan passes the small crowd and slows, staring at the open empty street beyond. He can't find the hydrant. He stops, and stares again, moves a bit further out into the street to look behind a tree, then it hits him and he turns back to the crowd, pressing through them with the hose, and arriving at the center knocks Ooper off the top of the fireplug.

"Look," Ooper yells, lying on the ground and pointing at Horgan, "an angel with power over fire." There is already a purple welt along his temple and cheek.

"Shut up, you," Horgan says, on his knees in front of the hydrant. The hydrant is the tiny Bicentennial Uncle Sam. His beard and smile are faded with the weather but his canvas trousers are still in fairly good condition. Horgan unbuttons them quickly and pushes them down. One of the women in the crowd giggles. Ooper and an old woman both shout "Filth" at the same moment. A prophylactic dangles, empty and limp, from the cap of the fireplug. Horgan utters an obscenity, removes the rubber, and tries to loosen the cap with his wrench.

Behind him, the same old woman shouts, "I got children, grandchildren, and great-grandchildren, and I won't have none of it, none of yours, stop scaring them, no, no, be patient, therefore, brethren, unto the coming of the Lord. Behold, the husbandman waiteth for the precious fruit of the earth, and hath long patience for it, until he receive the early and latter rain.''

"Put your foot on this wrench, somebody," Horgan yells.

"This is strange fire offered before the Lord," the old woman shouts, turning to each person in the crowd and nodding, smoothing the front of her slacks.

An upper floor crashes inside the burning house.

Horgan has his whole body curled on the ground in a spasm of effort, tugging on the wrench. Another woman, still in her house slippers, runs from the far side of the ring. Airborne, she lands on the end of the wrench. The cap turns. Horgan gets up and unscrews the cap the rest of the way, begins to attach the hose.

Ooper is up too, waving his hand at the fire, "The fire of the Lord fell, and consumed the Sacrifice, and the wood, and the stones, and the dust, and licked up the water.''

"No, no, He shall come unto us as the rain, as the latter and former rain unto the earth, my grandkids,'' the old woman throws back in the crowd's face.

Ooper and the old woman speak as if the crowd has to make up its mind on the spot or it will be too late. So when Horgan locks the hose in place and stands up, placing the wrench on the valve on top, he says, "You people make up your minds later. Right now get the hell away from my fireplug.''

"Need me?" the slippered lady asks, raising her foot and putting it on the wrench. Her offered toenails are a pale pink.

The crowd surrounding Ooper and the old woman moves a bit further down the street, arms folded and fingertips to lips, a tour group in a museum. Together

Horgan and the slippered woman, who is almost three inches taller than Horgan, crank the valve around. The water flushes through the big hose then to the Witherspoons, who surround the nozzle. They receive control of the water through the hose in the same manner that one receives control of a drop of mercury. They step three paces to the left with the pressure, then two paces to the right, and then six in a stumbling reverse. Horgan catches up with them then and together they direct a stream toward an upper window.

"Through the wrath of the Lord of Hosts is the land darkened, and the people shall be as the fuel of the fire."

"His doctrine shall drop as the rain, His speech shall distil as the dew, as the small rain upon the tender herb, and as the showers upon the grass."

"Can you hold this hose?" Horgan yells between the two old men.

"We've got her now, Horgan, yep."

Horgan lets go of the hose gingerly and backs away with his hands held open in the air, as if he's just balanced a plate on a ballpoint pen. As soon as he sees that it will stand, he turns back to the fire truck and switches on the pump to the five-hundred-gallon tank the truck carries. Then he climbs up to the cab and drives downwind. He moves to the house next door, jumps down, and reels out the hose. A woman there is standing in the thick smoke off of the Eckley house, trying to put out a fire in her gable that started when a bird's nest caught a cinder. Horgan pushes her, coughing, out of the way, turns the valve on the nozzle, and slams fifty gallons into the bird's nest and the flaming gable. He sprays down the rest of that end of the house to keep it cool. Then he turns and works on the grass fire approaching from the back of Miss Eckley's house. He fights it back behind the house and sees the whole rear of the house in flames, turns his hose on that for a moment, then realizes he's wasting water. It's gone, he thinks. She's burned her house down to keep me away from that elevator, he thinks.

He runs back through the smoke, dragging the hose, to calls from Whit.

"The next block down, Coach. Yard on fire."

"Therefore as the fire devoureth the stubble, and the flame consumeth the chaff, so their root shall be as rottenness, and their blossom shall go up as dust."

The crowd murmurs in assent, turning from Ooper to the wreck of the house, the huge, parched, shuffling crack of its falling.

The old woman shakes her head at them and at the old house. "Better is the end of a thing than the beginning thereof: and the patient in spirit is better than the proud in spirit. You're proud of yourself, Ooper."

And the old woman lays back and swings forward with her doubled fist, aiming at the wide white block of Ooper's forehead, but Ooper, twenty years younger, paper smothers rock, catches the fist in his two red hands and drags the old woman forward and whispers in her big drooping ear, "Thou shalt be for fuel to the fire. How it's going to be." Then lets the old woman go, and breaking free of the crowd, puts his hand to his swollen face and runs.

Horgan drives the fire truck slowly so that Whit, three women, and four other children can keep the hose from dragging on the pavement. They all stop every two or three houses and Horgan puts out a front or backyard fire. By the time they are three blocks away and have put out the last fire, two more have lit behind them. They move back slowly, the women and children lugging the hose.

I am here, Horgan thinks, and he climbs down from the cab, taking the nozzle from the wet, wind-blown women and children and showering a grass fire that has run up against a house and climbed a porch post. I am here, among women and children and old men, held hostage by an old woman who decides one morning to let the whole town burn down.

The Witherspoons back away from the house when it collapses, the heat billowing out into the street, and they and the crowd watch it burn. The three chimneys stand among the flames, and twisted pipes sway in the hot air. The copper sheeting of the roof warps and melts. Horgan and the rest of the crowd stand downwind in the thin smoke, stamping out cinders as they fall. The Witherspoons move back in toward the ashes slowly, with a fine spray. A bird begins to fly between the chimneys but the hot air there lifts him up and leaves again the waffling blue-ness of the heat and sky beyond. The heat is every-where and unapproachable, not just the heat of the fire but from the sky too and the reflecting pavement and earth. Most of the children are bare-chested and the women are down to their Saturday morning night-gowns, their housecoats flung and sprawling in yards and on sidewalks. The old men's shirts are dark with perspiration and the constant blowing spray from the fire hose.

Akton wails up, gets out of his patrol car slowly, and watches the dying of the fire with his hands at his side. After Horgan rolls up the fire truck's hose and stows it away, he goes to him.

"Where are my men?" he asks.

Akton folds his arms, bringing them up from his sides like pieces of short lumber. "Just listen here," he says, "next time you fool with me I'll crack your head too."

"Where are my goddamned men?" Horgan says. "Did you tell her it was her damned house on fire?"

"I told her. She said she couldn't spare them today."

"They're not hers to spare. They're mine. I hit the goddamned emergency siren. They were supposed to come. Look at that line of yards and houses. You almost burned down this whole town."

"That was Double-nought did that. It was just supposed to be the shack," Akton says.

"She did it," and Horgan stays quiet for a moment. "I was supposed to have an inspection out there today. She did it to keep me away, didn't she?"

Akton stands there, his arms still crossed. The stinging rises in Horgan's arms then and he looks down at them. "Did she even ask about her worthless cats? Is she gonna show up here at all? Did you tell her the house was BURNING DOWN?!"

"Said for you to clean up best you could. Said she didn't have time today."

"Well, you tell her there's nothing left to clean up." Horgan turns away, turns back. "No. I'll tell her that. You can tell her I'm coming as soon as I finish here."

Akton moves back to his car, opens the door. "You just don't fool with me, Horgan. Which way did Double-nought go? This is his fault."

A FLATLAND FABLE

"The chaff He will burn with fire unquenchable."
Horgan turns, without answering, to the old men
Witherspoon, who tramp and bend among the charred
and angled timbers, the thick ashes, of Miss Eckley's
house.

- 8 -

There is the heat off the engine and the heat in the memory of the fire and the sun blinding off the hood of the truck and the sun like a reproach on his bare arms and brow and the sun unforgivable for this moment. It is not hot, Horgan thinks. It is not hot.

Well, it is hot, he thinks, and what am I to say? I said nothing for the birds or for my father and of that said for the boys only timidly. I let her close a wooden door in my face. He thinks of the old woman yelling at his tall father, and drives too rapidly over the tracks of the Burlington-Northern. It knocks his hands from the wheel for a moment and the thud of the shocks bottoming out frightens him. Calm, Horgan, calm. Where will she find a bed tonight? Who in this town will give her a bed? Ooper perhaps, a cot in his tent. No, not now. Not with the house going up too. Her distraction turned disaster, yet not enough of a disaster to take her from the elevator. Akton maybe.

And he tries to imagine Akton stepping into the tin cubicle of her office to tell her the wind was high and that her house was burning, that she'd better let the volunteers go now, Horgan would need them to save the house. Tries to imagine it but stalls because he can't imagine a man telling a woman her house is on fire and the woman not even bothering to get up from the chair she's in. Not getting up and not walking even to the front of the desk, much less bolting to the resound of the tin door slamming, rushing to her burning house, even if it was just to watch it burn and fall in. Much less letting the volunteer firemen she hires go and help save the house her father built, the town's biggest house, that she has held private since his death and her takeover of the elevator, and which she must have known would have to be entered if she wasn't there to prevent it. Not even. But just sitting there at the news. Just watching the man bring it and probably not even bothering to send him away, maybe not even bothering to notice him in the first place, since whatever she was doing was far too important to leave for the burning of her home. Akton turning away from his non-reception and leaving as quietly as he could after telling her, probably holding onto the knob on the outside of the door to let the latch slide to softly, even though he wouldn't have been able to hear himself think for the noise of the elevator around him, the train droning off the platform. And Miss Eckley going on with whatever, deducting the house and all in it, retaining her men.

And why? Horgan understanding the distraction, Miss Eckley knowing about the burning of the shack in the vacant lot—Akton knowing she wouldn't let the volunteers come—but why not let them come when she learned of the house? And when Akton returned to tell her she must also have understood that Horgan knew and would follow the fire with his inspection anyway, would not postpone it as he might have done with the simple burning of the shack, another of Ooper's many arsons for the Lord to put out, his Saturday half-day over with. So either she wanted the house to burn, finding some reason in the wind and mishap, or she wanted him to simply fight it alone, finding some pleasure in that, or perhaps the time bought with the burning of the house would somehow clear her of whatever, or maybe she refused even to acknowledge the mistake, that she could misjudge the wind, and out of simple belligerence she decided to let her house burn to the ground. She let it burn the eyelashes from his face simply to prove she meant it to.

He had entered the house but found no decrepit cake, no foul body, only the biding dust of the ancient rugs, portraits, papers, and furniture. And found that the plumbing didn't work. Akton's rotting hose. It must have been broken for years. The water bottles were stacked against the walls, and the burned backyard revealed a worn path to the old outhouse. She hadn't let the plumber in. This and the darkness of the house, the fine stained glass of the front windows and door boarded up. The only light came in from the big plate glass windows on the sides and back of the house. But there had not been time to really look. The back room that looked like her office was already in flames, and then, then there was that cat. The singed cat that he'd fallen over.

Horgan winces, backhanding the sweat from the scratches of his cheek, and then wiping his hand across his pants. The cuts have stopped bleeding and now swell pink through the black of the ashes coating his arms and face. Tears run down his face—the wind and the irritation of the smoke—and as he pulls in to a stop in the white gravel lot across the railroad tracks from the elevator, he reaches up and rubs his eye sockets clean with his fists. Then he keeps his eyes closed till the dust of the gravel and his stopping clears.

The elevator is huge and blurry above him as he

opens his eyes. Even at this distance, a full three-hundred feet away, and the grain cars between him and the elevator, it towers above his imagination like a cloud, something unbelievable in this flat, dry place. He and the whole town have lived in its shadow since long before he was born, but the sight of it still unnerves him. The tower, the legs, spouts, hoppers, and other conveyors gleam in his blurred vision, and the birds wheel above it all, dim too, like birds wheeling within a gauze, wheeling in the smoke of the tears of his eyes. He rubs his eyes again, standing in the gravel, and looks up and then looks down, holding his cupped and cut palms to his face to stay the wind. His eyesight is fine. His eyesight is fine. There is no blurring. Among the white gravel are the splintered and broken bones of the birds. He looks back up at the elevator and sees that the blurring is tawny, a shade of chaff. The birds whirl in it before the blur is driven windward.

"Dust," Horgan says.

And for the first time he consciously notes the long line of the Burlington-Northern, the cars along the spur, and the grain trucks stacked and chugging diesel behind the facade of the elevator. There is the rigging of two temporary chutes. So she can unload and load at the same time, he thinks. Too much turnover and not enough ventilation. It's all in the air. If it's like this outside, what's it like inside. She wanted to trade her shack for a day's dangerous work.

He crosses a double set of tracks then climbs over the linkage between two empty cars. They jolt forward as he jumps off and Pilk, one of his volunteers and an older cousin of Sickopoose, catches him before he falls down off the second highest point in this country.

Pilk, twenty-six and one of Kidder's high school classmates, stands Horgan up. Pilk is covered in the dust of the elevator and his eyes and mouth open up out of a blank space of tan. He begins to explain even before Horgan can look at him.

"She almost fired me, Horgan. I tried to come but she caught me and said she'd fire me for sure so I had to say I was just going out to the car for my goggles. I told her I had something in my eye already."

Horgan stands in front of him, rubbing the knee he bumped on the linkage. He doesn't look at Pilk but above him, at the blurred and overshadowing elevator.

"She came out to each one of us individually early this morning and said if the siren was to go off we weren't to be bothered with it. Said you'd called and there was to be some work on it. You didn't call, did you, Horgan? We've already told her the dust was too high."

He shakes his head, watching the dust spew from the chutes and fall in eddies downward till it is caught by an updraft of wind or heat and is blasted into scattered and separate motes rising, falling, crossing, drifting. The dust falls about him and Pilk and suddenly the whole world becomes grainy, like an old, yellowed, and enlarged news photo. It makes him think of the burning wall in Miss Eckley's house again.

"I knew it, Horgan. So we didn't come when the siren went off but then we saw the flames, some of us did, and we gathered, meaning to leave, and she came out of her office and said there'd be no jobs to come back to for any who left, that it was her place burning and she could let it burn if she liked, and you know there's no other jobs in this town, Horgan. I need to live here close to my dad, Horgan. So we stood there a bit, but she stood there too, right with us, till we broke up and went back to work. I tried to get off a few minutes later but she was still there on the dock and so I had to deny it. You can see that. There wasn't anybody hurt?''

And Horgan, cooled by the dust, the veiled world, the talking, and the shadow of the elevator, and strangely cooled by his own disbelief, says, ''Wasn't anybody hurt.'' And he walks beyond Pilk.

He pulls and then pushes himself by his palms up on the concrete platform at the back of the elevator. The dust is thicker here; it is not dangerous yet, though, he thinks. There are men all over the platform, guiding the chutes, moving the trucks and cars through. She's got every able body in the county working here today, he thinks. He stands on the platform for a moment, then begins to move through the tangle of movement and noise. He notices the dust beginning to cling to the hair of his forearms. He ducks under a chute, sidesteps two men carrying shovels, and it is when he is within twenty-five feet of the tin office that he hears his ballplayers.

It is Witherspoon, Gaspar, Rutley, Rutley, Feeb, Yanks, all having fathers who work at the elevator who weren't going to be let off for the game, and Sickopoose himself, who Horgan knew didn't even have a father. His mother had taught him how to play ball, practiced with him. The boys are in a tight bunch, holding on to each other with their free and gloved hands. The foreman is trying to move them off the platform. The boys are yelling, and yell louder when they see Horgan. They don't seem to yell at him as much as for him. They yell up into the mote-soaked air, ''We want our fathers, we want our fathers,'' and they strike out from their pack with a baseball bat. The foreman jumps back. Gaspar steps out of the group then, horseapple in hand and already in his windup, and throws a strike at Miss Eckley's tin door. The horseapple smashes and explodes against the door, but no one comes out.

"All right, goddammit, that does it. You kids get out of here, now!" the foreman screams through the dust, and he advances.

The ballplayers collapse to the concrete and cover their heads. "Daddy!" they scream. The Rutley twins' father, with his shovel, comes at the foreman then from across the platform. He stops on the far side of the huddled ballplayers.

"You lay a hand on these boys..." and the father doesn't finish, but raises his shovel a little higher.

"Let our fathers go," Sickopoose screams.

"Coach!" Yanks yells, "Get her out here, Coach."

"She won't even come out, Coach," one of the Rutley twins says, pointing at the tin office.

His father says, "You be quiet, boy." And he lowers his shovel. He looks at Horgan. He is a volunteer too. "All you boys go on back home before you get your daddies in trouble. Go on now," Rutley says.

Horgan is by them now. He holds his hands out, palms down, the signal to hit the dirt, to slide. The boys stay on the ground. "I'm on my way to talk to her right now," he says. "Go on home. I'll do what I can. And don't be late for the pre-game practice. Go on home and eat a good lunch."

"We've been practicing, Coach. Just like you told us," the Rutley twins say in unison. The boys stand up, brushing the chaff from their pants.

The Rutleys' dad looks from them to Horgan, to

them and back at Horgan. "These boys woke me up at six this morning throwing a baseball on the roof. You tell them to do that?"

Horgan, ready to battle with Miss Eckley, doesn't want to slip to the defensive. It wouldn't be good preparation. "Your boys have dropped eleven balls this season because they came out of the sun." It was true he'd told them to practice this way, but it was also true that he'd warned them not to do it too early. But it wasn't the time or place to undermine them.

"We've all been practicing, Coach," Yanks says in the relative quiet that follows.

Then when it is apparent that they are going to have to leave, Witherspoon pokes his catcher's mitt up in the foreman's face, standing on tiptoe to do it, and says, "Fool with me again..." and he purposely leaves the sentence dangling in the dust. He sneers at the foreman as he turns, holds his fierce gaze on him, and hangs out at the back of the pack of ball-players till they're off the platform.

Horgan stands with Rutley as they go. "I'm sorry, Horgan," Rutley says, holding his shovel with both hands. "I forgot who I was mad at. I can't have the foreman after me. He might have Miss Eckley take my job."

"I'll see what I can do to get you and the others off for the game," Horgan says.

"You won't be able to do anything. We've been asking all week."

"It's okay," Horgan says, walking toward the galvanized shell of her office, "she owes me one."

"The fire, Horgan?" Rutley yells after him. "How'd the fire go?"

And Horgan, taking hold of the doorknob, does

not think of the fire, or Rutley or Miss Eckley, but sneezes greatly, turning his head to one side, then sneezes again, turning his head to the other side so as not to sneeze on his hand that holds the doorknob. And after he sneezes he holds still for a moment waiting for a third sneeze to strike but it does not come. Instead there is just an emptiness of the stomach and he thinks of Kidder and her SpaghettiOs. And this passes naturally to the emptiness of her stomach, Kidder's, and suddenly, without warning and self-inflicted, he is undermined. Before it can go any further he opens the corrugated door.

The dust blows in with him like snow. He stamps his feet even though it's over one hundred degrees outside. He stands there, holding the knob, trying to become accustomed to the darkness.

"Close the door."

He closes it.

"I won't give you many minutes," she says. "There's too much work for your interference today."

His pupils dilate and he finds her, standing behind the metal desk but still dwarfed by it, separating invoices. He thinks of Kidder again because he realizes she and Miss Eckley are of exactly the same height and build.

"You're going to have to make time for me today, Miss Eckley." And she doesn't look up or even pause so he adds, "Lady!"

She stops. "Did you save my house?" she says, in the same way you might say, "Did you make your bed?"

He does not know if he should go on, or just throw his hands up in the air and move to another town.

There didn't seem to be any sense in arguing. What he'd thought was steam in him was only smoke. He would give her a citation for the dust, the inadequate ventilation, but he couldn't make her shut down the elevator. He supposedly had the power, but even if he walked out on the platform and began yelling, waving the citation, it wouldn't cause the men to more than linger for a moment before they went on with their work. They had seen Akton there with her already this morning. Those who did walk off, if any would, would also lose their jobs, and there weren't any others in Eckley. Seventy-five men worked at the elevator. Everybody else in town was either a teacher or a farmer, or they worked at one of the few stores. He could contact the State Fire Board, but they couldn't take action for days.

"Your house is gone," he says.

"It was mine," and she halts for a moment, "it was mine to let burn."

"You almost burned down the whole town. You misjudged the wind. You meant to burn down that shack to keep me out of here till Monday. I guess you'll be done with all this work by Monday. But you burned down your house, lady. I put two old men and one hose on it but I had to fight fires downwind. Your house never had a chance. Without these men you kept here it didn't have a chance." Horgan tells himself to turn around and slam his fist into the tin door because his heart is not in his voice. He turns, and hits the tin, turns back, and says, "Why? Why didn't you let these men go? I know you've never personally cared for me but that's not enough reason to let your house burn down."

"You just shut up," she knifes out at him. "You

just shut your mouth. You don't know anything. You're just a boy. The house can be spared. These men can't."

And she stops. Horgan waits for her to go on but she is caught up in the papers of her desk, looking for something, a particular invoice.

"What?" Horgan says, "Why can't you spare ten men?"

"I'll have you go. I'm busy."

"Listen. I've got the smoke of your house all over me. I've got no hair on my face and little on my arms. I got a busted head and enough scratches... you talk."

"Have you seen a drop of rain in four months?" she says, slamming a stack of papers down on the desk top.

"What?"

"Have you seen a drop of rain in four months?"

"No!" he curses, exasperated.

"Neither have I. Neither has anyone else. Well, there hasn't been much grain grown either. Do you think this town would be here at all if it weren't for me and my elevator? This work today came along and I took it. It's got to be done today. They want it today. It's about the only work we've had all year. It's a drought, boy. It's a drought. I can't spare any men today. Neither your volunteers nor those boys' fathers. This elevator has to make it."

Horgan breaks in, "Don't ever..." But she doesn't stop.

"This place is alone with its weather. It's nothing but a flat place out of which to make something. And the only things that hold this country together are tin and barbed wire, and if we didn't nail the tin down anew every spring it would be gone by the fall, and if I were to snip three strands of barbed wire at a corner post the whole place would coil up and blow away like a tumbleweed. The only thing that's lasted, that's going to last, is this monolith, my elevator. After all the big cities are blown away with their bombs and the wind takes this town for good, it will still be here. It will be what Stonehenge is now. It will be a pyramid.''

''All they'll find,'' Horgan says, ''is another tomb, the fossils of men and birds. You need to shut this place down and you know it. A spark will go off and you'll kill every man here.''

''Then you leave,'' she says.

''I'll cite you.''

She looks at him, opens her purse at the side of the desk and takes out a twenty dollar bill. She holds the bill out to him. ''You run by the courthouse and pay it for me.'' He just stands there. She goes on, ''I've put in additional ventilation since that last thing with Dinks. I've turned off every unnecessary electrical circuit. Confiscated every cigarette.''

''Look,'' Horgan says, ''shut this place down; don't ever hold my men again; let these boys' fathers watch their last game; and for God's sake stop killing birds.''

''Let this town blow away,'' she adds.

''If that's what those things mean, then, yes,'' Horgan says. ''There's other places to be.''

''Get out,'' she says, ''you're a child.''

- 9 -

After he has showered, Kidder sits him down at their kitchen table and rubs his cuts with alcohol. He has the scratches on his cheek and down the length of his arms, on the backs and palms of his hands, but also a long swipe down his side.

"Didn't you have your coat on?" she says, dipping a cotton ball.

"Didn't have time," he says.

"Horgan! What about your helmet?"

Horgan reaches up and feels the bump on the back of his head.

"I guess I forgot," he says.

"Listen," she says, and by the next word her voice has already cracked, "you're supposed to wear that stuff." And by the second sentence her nose is running. "I don't have to sit here and take this. You're all beat up." And by the beginning of the fourth sentence the water is rolling from the corners of her eyes. "You could have been dead in that house saving cats and left me here alone."

Horgan takes the cotton ball from her fingers and rubs the bruise on his knee. He doesn't look up at her. It takes him the better part of two minutes to stop rubbing the bruise and looking at it, trying to focus on its colors. He'd started to get foggy-eyed again, the stinging returning, but refusing to let it go any further made him want to explode with the pressure. It was not his fault that she would be alone. He was doing his best.

Kidder uses another cotton ball. There are scratches on his ankles too. She rubs on his ankles and wipes the tears from her cheeks with the back of her hand. "Of course she didn't ask about her cats," she says. "She saw your scratches. Anyway, the only reason she ever let them hang around was because they didn't need her."

"Didn't need her?" he says.

"They didn't need her. Most cats don't need anyone. They can take care of themselves. Leave a dog out and he'll starve in a week. A cat will make it."

"No, that's not right," Horgan says, lifting up and looking at her finally, "It's all a put on, it's just an air of self-assurance they have. They really need you. That's why I hate them. They won't admit it. I've always allied myself with the dogs."

Kidder shakes her head. "Anyway, her cats needed you."

"See," he says, "and look at the appreciation they showed," and he holds his hands out.

"What did you want?" she asks.

"I wanted ... I want ..." he starts, then stops.

"What?"

"I'm not a cat," he asserts, formidably. "I'm a dog. I've coached a ball team for seven years that's going to get squashed in the championship game for the seventh time. I did my best to save the house and pets of a lady who couldn't have cared less. And you're not so much worried about me as you are the possibility of me getting killed without you being pregnant."

Kidder, standing at the stove stirring the pot of SpaghettiOs, turns and flings the pot, SpaghettiOs, spoon, and all, against the kitchen wall over Horgan's head. She holds the fingers of one hand to her mouth, looking at him, and starts to walk from the room but ends up running. The SpaghettiOs slide down the white wall like huge white blood cells.

Horgan takes his forearm from his eyes and picks up the spoon at his feet. He sighs, stands up, and walks around the kitchen till he notices the gas burner. He reaches down and turns off the fire. "Thanks," he mumbles. Kidder is back in the doorway to the kitchen then, her eyes still red but no shaking in her voice.

"You take that back," she says. "You take it back right now."

"I take it back," he says, turning the gas knob on and off. "I didn't mean that at all. I'm just tired of being useless. I just want to be effective at something."

"Don't ever say anything like that again."

"All right," he says.

Kidder, knocking the counter lightly with her closed fist, slams it once hard. Then she rubs the little finger on that hand and says, "I bought two cans of SpaghettiOs. Get away from that stove."

Horgan moves slowly back to his chair at the table. His white towel that he's been wearing since his shower almost slips off on the way but he catches it.

Kidder wets a dish towel and cleans up the mess, starts a new pot of SpaghettiOs. Horgan doesn't breathe.

"Your ballplayers appreciate you," she says, finally, and he breathes again. "And I appreciate what you did today. I like cats. They're soft."

I love you, Horgan thinks. I've always wanted someone like you to love. But he doesn't say this. He says, instead, "Like babies." Kidder doesn't turn away from the stove this time. But after a moment her shoulders move and Horgan knows she is crying again. So he goes on with it. "You've already had yourself checked, haven't you? I mean about problems with having a baby. And you're okay, aren't you?"

"Yes," she says, "but that doesn't mean that you're not." She bangs the spoon on the rim of the pot and pours two bowls of SpaghettiOs. "The thing is to go on and not worry about it too much and your life will move along all right," she says, sitting down and pushing Horgan his bowl. "I've still got this month to see about this evening."

"You haven't been throwing up," Horgan says.

"Everybody doesn't do that, Horgan," and she pushes the snot back up her nose with the heel of her palm, sniffing. "The excitement in our lives comes from quarters we don't even consider. That's what makes it exciting: that we never even imagined. Things happen to you when you least expect them."

"Well, in that case you're always blindsided."

Kidder slams her spoon down and yells, "A watched clock doesn't tick!"

"It does too!" he yells back.

They both sit there, looking down into their bowls.

"I'm sorry," he says. "I'm sorry."

"It's true," she says, "I do want a baby. Awful bad."

"I know."

"I think about it all the time. What it will be like."

"I know."

"I think about names, and when to start teaching it to read and everything."

"I know."

"Let's not talk anymore about it. Let's wait till tonight. I'm worn out."

Horgan turns in his chair, rolls his spoon in his lunch, thinking, and if I am unable, asking, "Are you okay? I mean, are you happy? I mean ..."

"Why, Horgan." She pauses. "Yes. You take that back too. Aren't you?"

"I'm happy with you. I love you so much. I've always wanted someone like you to love. It's me I'm not so sure about. It's all come upon me lately. I used to be all right. But I don't know. I don't think I'm too old to become reconciled to my life."

Kidder leaves her spoon in the bowl. "Reconciled? That's not it, Horgan. You're reconciled to your life, honey. What you're not reconciled to is dying."

"I'm only forty," he says, "I don't think about it."

"I'm only twenty-six, and I think about it. I think about it mostly because of the baby though."

"I don't want my dad to die," he says.

"I know, honey."

"I mean all he's ever had is me and he'll miss ..."

"Horgan."

"First of all, it just isn't fair."

"Horgan, honey."

"Now, I'm not, and I'm not going to right now. Please come here."

And Kidder gets up and goes to him, sits in his lap after he backs away from the table.

"Honey," Kidder says, her arms around his neck, "that's one thing. Your dad didn't have anything wrong with him. Here you are."

And Horgan says, simply, "Un hunh," but his mind becomes airy, porous, with the obvious and beautiful truth of Kidder's insight.

"And you were born when he was in his thirties, right?"

"Un hunh," Horgan mumbles, his heart dissolving in oxygen. Ventilated ventricles. All the smoke and dust in him is taken up. A fan blows across his face. Horgan says, very loudly, "He sure was!"

Kidder picks at the towel hanging over Horgan's bruised knee and says, "Let's go," in his ear.

"What?" Horgan says.

Then he says, "Oh."

And then, "Let me finish my SpaghettiOs first."

"Okay." And she jumps off his lap. "I'll be in the bedroom. I love you."

Horgan says, "He sure was," and picks up his shining spoon.

- 10 -

Horgan finishes his lunch, rinses the bowl and spoon, and starts toward the bedroom holding his white towel. The house darkens as he walks from the window garnished kitchen through the living room and hallway to Kidder. She has drawn all the shades and turned out the light. Horgan walks and thinks of sliding in darkness, the worn and smooth slide fire escape at the middle school. This is my home, he thinks, passing the clothes hamper in the hallway. My father lived here. I'm going to Kidder. Someone save me in my love for her.

Horgan's father lies in the hollow of himself. The nurse holds the bone ball of his shoulder as she pulls gently on the clear tube down his throat. The end comes clear but leaves a drop of blood on his pale lower lip and then another drop on the white sheet.

"Breathe a little easier now?" she asks, smiling, holding the end of the oxygen tube in her fist.

Horgan's father nods.

She turns to Dutton then and says, "You make sure he doesn't try to talk."

"Yes, ma'am."

"Do you want a lunch? He's having his now." And she smiles again and touches the IV bottle.

"Yes, ma'am, I'll have lunch again today. It's

meatloaf on Saturdays. I like hospital food," Dutton says.

"I think he does breathe easier without the oxygen." And she reaches down with one hand and touches the spot on his lip and in the same motion pushes back a wisp of hair straggling over his forehead.

Horgan's father nods.

When she leaves he moves his arm, the cavity of his shoulder, the shallow wrist, and the trough of his hand out from underneath the sheet and writes. He writes, "I feel sorry for myself."

And Dutton takes the card from him. He is the huddled shoulders of a big man in a little chair. He takes the card and turns it over and over in the soft pads of his hands.

The fan is up on a stool at the foot of the bed when Horgan gets there. And Kidder is in her white T-shirt, sitting on the side of the bed. It is all her legs can do to get her feet to the floor. Her hair is out of the tight braid of the morning and falls over one shoulder in front, but it still retains the curves and wrinkles of the braid. Her hands gather between her thighs, holding the T-shirt tightly there, and tautly in a line to her neck. It is the upward curve of the underside of her breast, showing dark faintly through the white shirt, and the air passing over her lower lip, and the doubled hem of the shirt along her thigh that excite him. She kicks off the floor and pushes herself up, scooting backward to the headboard and leaning there. The hem of the shirt rests along the junction of her abdomen and thighs now, rests in the very thickness of her hair there, covering only the thin line of faint auburn down that leads to her navel. Horgan hangs his towel on the corner of the footboard so she won't have to waddle to the bathroom later, and then he crawls into the bed. She slides down, slowly, on her back as he does this, and so he watches the glistening revealed as she does this, the slight arch of her back and the delicateness of her spreading thighs, the bend of her knee as it skims across the sheet. He moves between her legs on his knees, and without touching her, leans over, his hands on the pillow on each side of her head, and kisses her. And moving back, above her, still without touching her, as the muscles of her stomach pull taut and her knees straighten, her legs stretching out, moving back, he stops and lets his face fall to her, not working her or stroking her as she pivots her hips and opens to him, but pressing there, the heave of his breath, pressing and spreading her, moving in her, the wetness on his face, the heaviness and salt, moving in, pressing, not breathing, not breathing, pressed to and between the warmth and tight and wet of her, thinking, let me in, breathe for me.

The day in this country so long, so obstinate, that the moon blunders into it from behind like some startled old woman in line. Her faint light, mottled water color blue, is an apology. Eckley is brighter, reflects more light and heat, than she does. The town is a hot place on the hot of the flatness, shards of light, shocks of chrome, and all wavering in its own false water, wading in its mirage. There are awnings, shades, coddled leaves, arcing fans and the constant whine of the air conditioners in the whine of the wind, a cool glass of water brought from three hundred feet below, cotton shirts, and people avoiding the heat of each other's bodies, but nothing and no one overcoming the season, the era, their species. The sunwhipped city is burnished, burnished.

Shrugsby, knowing Pillsneck and fearing the worst, hitches a ride on the Route back to his grandfather's farm. He checks the barn first, then the house, then looks out across the fields for smoke. But Pillsneck isn't there. He sighs a sigh of relief, then says aloud, "Then where is he with those matches?" And he trots all the way back out to the Route, and hitches another ride back into town.

"It's time to be beyond that," Dutton says, setting the card back up on the edge of the bed. "Other things should have taken the place of that; it's been so long. You're just tired right now. You're not sorry for yourself because of this sickness now, are you?"

Horgan's father shakes his head no.

"Well, this sickness is a better thing to be sorry for than that thing is," Dutton says. "What happened to you happens to everybody to some extent. You just took it harder than most."

Horgan's father writes, "Sorry for Horgan too."

Dutton takes it. "Well, I am too, a little. But Horgan never was. I know he was and is much better off as a result of it all. But with your sickness he needs to know now. He'll understand."

He writes, "Don't say all," and then, on another card, "Please. I am his father."

"Joe, now," Dutton says, but holds off. "Okay, I'll just say the rest."

And they both are silent, till the tray comes for Dutton, and he says, "Look here. Look here, Joe."

He rises up after a moment, and lays his warm cheek on her wet hair, her hips still shuttling and rolling, and he feels the pulse of her blood through the mound of her hair, skin, and bone. He lifts up a bit more, cradling her lower back in his arms and kissing along the dramatic flair of her hips, pushing the shirt up. She turns in his arms, and turns back while he moves up her, taking the soft underside of her breast in his mouth, then the nipple and he hears her when he does this, her yearning all too blatant, but enjoying it still, the sucking, sucking his life out of her but never sucking enough, somehow unable to draw deeply enough, thinking, her beauty, her beauty mine, white white white white in my mouth and he comes up, notices the reddening of her under his lip, cheek, and chin and he drops again, drawing from her. She spreads her legs as wide as they will and lifts up, wrapping them around the back of his thighs, and Horgan, knowing he is ready, feeling his hardness and wanting her, pauses under her ear as he moves up to her, thinking if I am unable, and then he is there, among her.

Ooper rests in the unbearable heat of his tent. He rubs his bruised face, crying with anger, searching for something cool to put on it, but ends up throwing and kicking, falling on the floor of the tent and beating the earth. "It's true," he cries, softly, "It is true! The Lord Jesus, it's true, shall be revealed from heaven, with his mighty angels, in flaming fire, taking vengeance on them that know not God, and that obey not the Gospel. It is true!" And he rises up onto his knees. The suit, he finds under his cot, and although it is wool and searing, he puts it on. He takes up his gas can then, and leaves the tent, tying the flap carefully back together. "Oh, Jesus," and he can't seem to stop crying, "Oh, Jesus, help me. I'm trying to be good."

Even when it rains the sun shines here. The sky is more often than not simply too big for a cloud to cover it. A darkness on the horizon and you think of not land but water. But a darkness of the summer is usually the dust coming, dust in a billowing wave to add more dust to the present and accumulated dust. Or it, the darkness, is night coming, visible as any storm. Night approaches, at last, as no secret.

Horgan's father watches Dutton eat. He watches him eat while he works at the cards, writing, telling a long story, piling them in a stack on the bed near his sunken belly. He puts, at most, five big words to a card. He writes and writes, moving his cupped palm over the paper, and as he writes a memory is born and he smiles. He smiles at each of the cards as he lays them aside. When Dutton finishes eating, Horgan's father hands the story to him.

Dutton takes them, says, "A mouthful," and smiles at him.

"Remember. School. The four of us at the exhibition game. I would make a pitch and look up at her in the stands. I pitched my best. We did it. I enjoyed so much looking at her in the stands. Pretty."

Dutton reads the cards, then puts them in the drawer with the others he is saving. He rises, moves about the small room, and looks out the window at the open blue sky, the town itself, the Route, and in the distance the elevator and its birds. He turns back to the bed and sits down again. "She was never," he says, "at any one moment of her life, a better person than you. I have always refrained from saying that because I knew you wouldn't want me to but I've said it now, and I won't say it again. She left a better man than she'd ever know, in you and Horgan. There."

And Horgan does not so much thrust as he does draw himself up into her, as she draws herself around him, and draws deeply on the air at his shoulder and draws deeply. He puts his hands under her back and reaching up from behind grasps her shoulders, holding her steady while he pulls out and then allows himself to be drawn back, slide back, sucked into her body that turns at his touch. Her hips swoon in the sheets as he rocks. He lets go of her shoulders and reaches back, lifting her up with one hand, then the next, under her rear and holding on tightly to the taut wetness there and not stopping his movement, rising and falling in the bowl of her pelvis. And then, with the pleasure, and her whispering, he doesn't allow the suction but forces it, stroking into her and holding her tighter, leaning down and biting into the flesh of her breast and then straining for the nipple again and taking it erect into his mouth and still stroking below and squeezing and he thinking, if I am unable, her empty belly, blood month after month, if I am unable, and I would not blame her if I am unable she will leave me even with her love for me.

The ball team, including the two Norblunks, sits against the outside wall of the Phillips 66 station, drinking pops. Only Pillsneck and Shrugsby are missing.

"Wonder how Coach did with Miss Eckley?" Sickopoose wonders, his tongue, lips, and everything within a two-inch radius of his mouth a deep glowing orange.

Feeb, beating on his dark glove with a tire iron, says, "Can't believe her durn house burn down and her not want to see it. If she'd wanted to see it we probably would have followed her and seen it too."

"Coach was nasty lookin'," Gaspar says.

"Anybody seen their bus yet? I bet they're all five and a half feet tall," Whit says, and they all look at him.

Yanks says, "Well, how long till practice?" And he waves his bat in the air with a fiendish twist.

Norblunk is practicing tossing the ball to his brother from his glove. "Another couple hours or so."

Witherspoon says, "Well, if Pillsneck and Shrugsby don't show up soon... well, I'm tired of waiting. I'd play right now."

It is then that Shrugsby pops out of a car, screaming. He screams, "Fellas, fellas, that crazy fool's out there somewhere with a box of matches, says he's got to get Coach's attention. Fellas!"

"Double-nought?" they all ask.

"Pillsneck," Shrugsby answers.

"Maybe it was him burned down Miss Eckley's house," a Rutley suggests.

"Oh, my God!" Shrugsby screams.

"No, that was Ooper," Whit yells. He is the center of attention.

He is the center of attention till Shrugsby takes it, screaming, "Maybe they're out there together!"

And he holds it for perhaps three whole seconds before Ooper himself, filling his can at one of the gas pumps, takes it for good. Ooper notes the boys and he yells toward them, his voice a hand from underneath the bed. "Baseball," Ooper yells, "there's a false idol, for one." The boys fall apart and scramble, then come back together.

"The law's after you, Ooper," Whit yells back at him.

Witherspoon steps in front of Whit then. He holds his catcher's mitt up, the signal for a conference. They all gather on an imaginary pitcher's mound. Whit stands on the outside of the huddle on tiptoes, hitching up his pants again and again. One of the Norblunks says, "You're hurtin' my arm." Then they break out of the mound conference and head as the crow flies for Horgan's house. Ooper watches them go. When he screams again the boys run.

And suddenly the pleasure is too intense to think, to even move, to know only his love for her, to hold tightly, and try to remember to breathe. Kidder, in an obvious attempt to say his name as she arches her back fully, says, "Horg," and trails off, but Horgan takes it for the huskiness of her voice in the heat, and the action at hand and his mind calls it an attempt at another word and he says, holding her, "Yes, honey, yes, enjoy it; me too." And she falls back into the bed, at first wondering, then giggling, and finally having to roll out from underneath him to laugh without his weight on her stomach and chest.

She says, "I was trying to say your name, not 'orgasm,' honey," and she sits up to laugh with him and sees the red in his eyes from his thinking and so she stops and says, "Honey, don't worry, don't worry," and she looks down at the white sheets at their wet place, then puts the towel between her legs. "See," she says, "I'm still not bleeding. It could be right now."

"I'm not worried," he says, "but what if..."

"Neither am I. Please let's talk about it after the ball game." She stops then, stands up with the towel between her legs, and Horgan sees her mind hiding.

Pillsneck sets the fire now, lighting the taller grass under each of the three bleachers at the ballfield. When they are all burning well, and it doesn't take long, he runs back out to the pitcher's mound to wait for Horgan, his glove on his hand, and three baseballs at his feet.

Dutton gets up from the chair. "I'll go now," he says. "I won't come back to see you with Horgan.

But he'll understand what I tell him. I promise you he'll understand. I've got to get Shrugsby and take him to get his shirt and cap, then I'll go talk to Horgan. I'll come back for lunch tomorrow. Okay?''

Horgan's father nods.

And Dutton nods too, leaning on the frame of the door for a moment as he goes.

"Sex," Horgan says, "is like trying to get between a squirrel and his tree." He stands in front of the mirror in the bathroom holding one eyelid up and looking as far back into his head as he can.

"You're a queer puppy, honey," Kidder says, resting on the toilet.

So Horgan sings, "I love Kidder, I love Kidder, yes I do, yes I do," to the tune of "Frère Jacques" several times. He goes back into the bedroom after his examination and puts on some shorts, snapping the waistband, and his old white baseball pants from high school. They are worn and washed and just right, he thinks. I tried to play, he thinks.

"Go get 'em, honey," Kidder yells from the toilet. Then she runs out and drapes her T-shirt over his head. "Here, wear this for good luck. You still gonna go see your dad first? You have the time?"

"Sure," Horgan says.

"Tell him I'll be in later."

"I will."

"Tell him I love his heart."

"Okay."

"Goochie goochie goo," she says, grabbing his ribs.

And he is holding her close when the red phone rings again.

- 11 -

From afar he understands it is no false alarm. His ballfield burns. His truck bounces again over the tracks of the Burlington-Northern, but passes the elevator amid its haze of seed and chaff, and drives beyond, down the red dirt road through the dry fields to the ballfield. The diamond is only a half-mile from the elevator, is almost reached by its long shadow in the summer evenings. The three sections of bleachers burn still down their upper planes, while the grass beneath has only its smoke left. The wind has taken the grass fire from underneath the stands, through the chain link backstop and dugouts, and into the infield, and jumping the red dirt of the baselines, burns into the outfield, where it now moves on. The flames of the grass fire are too low and faint even to be seen in the bright day. There is only the blackness left behind and the sudden whiteness of the smoke springing from the earth.

Pillsneck stands on the mound of red dirt in the black of the infield. When he sees that Horgan has noticed him he stops working at his smoke-reddened eyes and begins throwing balls at a mitt he's tied to the backstop. He pitches in the white thickness of smoke skimming across the flat ground from the bleachers.

Horgan watches him for a moment, watches the first three throws driven into the palm of the dangling mitt, then thinks, he could win it possibly, and thinks concurrently, he set this fire. He jumps down from the truck, reels out the hose again, and uses the last of his water to put out the bleachers. The bottom step on each set has burned through in the middle and the ends rest in the black grass. The upper seats are charred and still smoke as the water runs and drips off. Horgan tests each board, stepping up and bouncing. You can still sit on them, he thinks. They'll still hold people. Then he takes his burlap sack and moves into the outfield. Standing in the already burnt, he slaps at the low flames. He brings the sack up over his shoulder and comes down, the smoke flaring away and avoiding his swing but the earth taking it full force and the flames nowhere to go but out. Black motes and grass cinders rise up around him as he moves along the fire line, leaving a red trail of footprints. He scrapes the ground with his sneaker and it bleeds, scars. Brings the now hot sack down again and again, the motion becoming rhythmical, putting out a fire becoming no more of an operation than hoeing, stopping an encroaching weed. Brings the hot sack up over his shoulder, grazing his cheek, up over his shoulder and it stalls there for a moment, like a flag, stalls and snaps flinging off smoke and burnt blades, then comes forward and down again, arcing over his shoulder. Horgan leaves his trail of red listening to the pop of the baseball in the leather. The wind carries it to him. And when he finishes the fire, and there is just the sparse smoke left, and the wind carrying off the burnt grass, the ground cover, exposing the earth beneath, he turns to the boy, walks to him.

Pillsneck holds his last ball till Horgan is close enough to watch but not close enough to stop his windup and pitch. He grips the ball along the seams with his first two fingers and withdraws into his windup, rolling his body like a satellite, rolling till his summer taut boy's body reveals each rib and tendon, and when he can withdraw no further he stops. And then coming loose. Pitching the way a normal person would blink, all reflex, as if he were being born. Or, and, pitching, coming loose, like a madman out of a coma. The ball leaves his hand in the torque of his snapped wrist and leaves spinning but straight, straight and hard at the batter's box, and Horgan thinks for a moment, well, maybe it wasn't the glove I heard him hitting, maybe it was something else, because this ball would kill a boy if there was one there at the plate, thinks this for a moment, waiting for the clang and rattle of the ball off the chain link, till the ball with the action of a snake dips down and left just before the plate and crosses its center and there is the pop of the ball against the pocket of the leather mitt. Strike. He had thrown a curve.

And Horgan, again for a moment, abandons his hope for rain and acknowledges the possibility of actually winning. But by the time he's to Pillsneck, he has the boy by his pitching arm and is saying, "You want to ruin your arm? You want to tear the joints out of it and not be able to throw a kiss? I told you," Horgan says loudly, "I told you not to try throwing curves. You're too young. You'll mess up your arm and not be able to play later."

"But we can win, Coach," Pillsneck says, "we can win. I can throw that pitch every time and they'll have ducked and backed out of the box by the time the ball crosses the plate."

"No," Horgan says.

"Coach!"

"No," Horgan says.

"Coach, we can win."

"Even if it was your turn I wouldn't let you throw that pitch. It's not your turn. It's Gaspar's. You've had your turn. It's Gaspar's. You've had your turn."

"But, Coach," and Pillsneck throws his glove out toward center field, "what's the use of playing if you've already had your turn?"

And Horgan, thinking at all times that he hasn't yet had his own turn, is always wishing for his own turn, had another picture of the bleakness of getting his wish, the afterwards of accomplishment. Pillsneck had his turn and won. He'd won all of his games and won the game that got them to the championship. All Horgan can think to say, after thinking that perhaps he has had his turn and just missed it, all he can think to say is, "You can't have your turn and someone else's too. You can't have two turns. You're not going to sit on the bench, anyway. You're going to play the whole game at first base. You can still hit."

"We can win, Coach. I can win it for you and they'll all believe. We've never won before. Why do you want to lose?"

"I don't want to lose, Pillsneck."

"It's the only thing that can happen, Coach."

"No, it's not. You can hit a homer. And Yanks might pull us through. And Gaspar isn't bad. He tries hard. He's won four out of six games." Horgan tries to put his hand on Pillsneck's shoulder but the boy flings it aside.

"My dad, Coach. I want to pitch for my dad. He's going to be here to watch."

"Go home," Horgan yells at him, "right now. And don't be late for practice. And if I ever see so much as a single match in your hand I'll bust your butt good. You've ruined this field. Go home."

And Horgan walks away from him, toward the fire truck, the burlap bag over his shoulder. Pillsneck runs to the backstop and picks up the balls, tears the mitt from the fence. When Horgan looks up from coiling the fire hose, the boy has picked up his glove from center field and is running toward town.

He finishes with the hose and throws the blackened sack up into the truck, then walks back to the charred bleachers. The smoke is gone now and most of the water he sprayed over them has already evaporated. He sits down on the second step up and rests his feet on the burned through bottom board.

I should be on my way to my father.

He sits there, at first wiping the sweat from his forehead, but after a moment letting the wind do that, just using his fist to hold up his sagging mind. The wind sings through the chain link of the backstop and the wind hums over the cracked boards he sits on. Whit's lumber has caught fire at last, he thinks.

The ballfield beyond is a patchwork of black on red. White baselines slant out into this, through the red and faintly into the black and then are lost in the outfield. Horgan rises, and walks around the near dugout and into left field. He kicks at tiny pieces of foil, a bottle cap, chafes smooth a small hump of dirt and knocks off the edges of old snake holes, filling them in. His steps leave red marks again, and wherever he chafes the wind takes the burnt leaves and carries them off. He walks back toward the infield, leaving now black marks in the red dirt as he crosses the baseline. He approaches the pitcher's mound as if it is a fresh grave. It rises above the lay of the land.

This is my father's field.

He steps up on the mound, places his toe on the white rectangle of rubber. The pitcher's mound is the highest point of land in this country. Horgan steps up and feels like he can see forever, to the very end of his life.

I should be on my way to my father.

His father, and this was more from Dutton, had come to Eckley, and before he did anything, find a place to live, get a job, a shave, take a piss, before he did anything, he began to organize a baseball team. It was in the time when baseball truly was America's sport, and every town, no matter how small, had a men's hardball team. During the time when every office and factory in the cities had hardball teams. There were ballplayers everywhere. But not in Eckley. And so Horgan's father organized a team, garnered one of the flat spots a half-mile from the elevator, and with his groundskeeper skills built a ballfield. He laid out the diamond and dug a hole in another field for the dirt to build the pitcher's mound. He put a fence behind home plate but there wasn't enough money for one around the outfield. So there were no automatic homers. It was how far you could hit it and how fast you could run. He'd planted, originally, the hardiest grass he could find in the outfield and infield, but even that wasn't hardy enough for the sun and wind, and over the years the hardy weeds came, and he called that grass and kept it mowed at one inch.

The Eckley men's team lasted four years, till the war took most of the players. They played every town in the surrounding counties. The four trophies are there still in the town hall. By the time the war was over the pitcher's mound and the bases had been moved in toward home plate by almost forty feet. A gang of boys had taken a wheelbarrow out to the field one night. And so Horgan's father, nearing his fortieth birthday, started the boy's team. Horgan was his right fielder. He played for an inning late in the game.

So Horgan played on the field as a boy and all through high school with his love for the game. But he soon realized that what his father had, he hadn't received. His father kept him in the best gloves and equipment money could buy, practiced with him day and night, talked baseball over lunch and dinner, but he hadn't given him his height, his long arms and fingers, his coordination. Horgan received only his love for the game. And coupled with his inability, his love produced only frustration after frustration: bench time, low batting averages, errors. So he played in the hot sun, his back peeling, chasing bad hops, living for the occasional solid and pure feel of the ball off his bat, the thump in the pocket of his glove. And these were enough. These and his father in the bleachers watching.

I should be on my way to my father.

I do not want to lose.

Whose turn is it?

My father has had his turn.

Wait for your turn.

You can't have a turn.

I do not want to lose.

Kidder, Kidder, Kidder.

Father, why must.

Father, why.

A FLATLAND FABLE

The ball feels swell off his bat, and he runs in the wonder of the ball rising over the outstretched glove of the second baseman and runs, almost wanting to run after the ball off of his bat, feeling that tug of ownership as he rounds first base, the ball dropping to the red earth in right-center field and skidding on beyond, a puff of dust off the scrabble, and the two fielders converging on it, closing in, run, Horgan, run, and rounding second, trying to beat the equation of ball and home plate, he glances up momentarily and sees a giant in the sky, alone up there, recognizing his father after another step, standing on the top step of the bleachers and waving him home. So he runs. Runs watching his father instead of the baseline and trying to turn third he catches it wrong. The base holds his foot while his ankle turns. And he falls out, rolls over the base, his body over his body—body earth body earth—and stopping amid the red dust, slamming into the chain link. Thinking then, get up, get up, and trying that but the ankle not trying, folding like a lawn chair. The ball retrieved and coming in all the time as he tries to get up, inches toward home, the ball sooner than he can believe back to where it started and the catcher, leaning over, thoughtfully, softly, touching him on the shoulder.

Horgan, standing on the mound, visibly drops and draws back his shoulder, puts his hand there so powerful is the memory. I'm so, he thinks, I'm so... He steps down off the mound, surprised that his ankle holds under his weight.

What do you do if you've already had your turn? He thinks of his father, missing for his mother his turn, waiting for another, watching his son round third base on his shoulder. His father, waiting and waiting on his wife to return. His father who was the pitcher's mound and the hole it was made of.

I should be on my way.

He looks over the burnt field and out and beyond, to the elevator, clouded in dust and birds. It wavers in the heat, but its shadow moves steadily over the fields toward him.

There must be, somewhere, something I can do something about. Fire, his father, dust and birds, an old woman, a young woman, a team of boys, a bunch of men.

He moves toward his fire engine, then stops to wait. Out of the shadow and dust of the elevator comes another dust, moving quickly toward him. Dutton along the dirt road toward him.

Out of his old truck, walking hugely across the ground, Dutton says, "I've been searching for you. Your house is full of boys. Kidder's taking care of them. They've all got a pop and a potato chip." Taking Horgan under his great sagging arm and leading him back to the burnt bleachers.

- 12 -

"Your father in his prime, he was devoted," Dutton says, deeply. He is a red old man, red as the soil of this country, who eats many eggs. Whiskers, white stubble, spring from his face like smoke. He sits on the black bleachers, elbows on knees, his hands moving in the air. The wind blows a few strands of hair down over the flatness of his broad and creased forehead. "And I was his friend."

Water starts from his eyes and Horgan thinks of the wind and then thinks again. The wind is at his back.

"He's all right, Dutty?"

"I've been to see him."

"He's all right?" And Horgan starts to get up.

"He's okay, Horgan, son. He's okay. He's worse today than yesterday. But you know it's been that way for a while."

And Horgan rises again. "Well, I ought to be on my way then."

"Don't go," Dutton says. "Don't go. It was me called in that false alarm this morning. I did it."

Horgan sits back down on the cracked board and looks at the old man. Dutton does not look up. Looks down at the space of bleacher between his feet. Horgan sits down, and reaching up, pets him on the shoulder.

"What?" Horgan says, watching the precious water fall from Dutton's face to the space of bleacher, watching it spread and then be taken up by the wind and heat.

Dutton, the weight of his great body bending the bleacher, his forearms and hands moving in the air. "I'm real big and I'm ashamed that I worry about living with this alone."

Birds stall above them and come to rest in a line on the top pipe of the backstop. The birds are brown and small.

Horgan waits. He waits in his exhaustion, not looking up, not concentrating on the sun on his back.

"But I'm still not going to. I've talked it over with your daddy and he says it's fine, it's the thing to be done. So I need to talk to you here for a while, and then you're to go to your daddy.

"It was me made that phone call about my barn. Wasn't one of the boys. I was trying to talk to you in a way you wouldn't notice. I'm old and I don't know that I think straight sometimes. Me and your father both wonder how we got to be seventy. We were both twenty-five just yesterday. I can't explain it to you."

"I understand," Horgan says.

"The thing is your daddy still thinks of you as a baby, just a boy, like my little Shrugsby. But that's not so, is it, and I've convinced him of that, and so all of this is my idea, my responsibility, and if you see it at last as wrong, then it's me you should reproach. Don't reproach your old daddy. He's a scared man in his love. This is all long overdue, but he's gotten worse today like every day, and it's come time for it, and he is my old friend, and I love him, and I love you, and I don't know any other way around it than to tell it.

"And I have been thinking about how to tell it for a long time, how to tell you about your momma, and your daddy, because I always felt it would come down to me at last, knowing them both. One of them never would and the other couldn't. I think from the very start this was set down as my job, to pass things on."

"The way you go on maybe I don't want to know," Horgan says. "I don't want to hear anything against Dad now. He don't deserve it, and I don't want to hear it, even from you, Dutty. I need to get up from here."

"Don't go," the old man pleads, "it's nothing against him. But you've got to hear it. It's important. It's what's going to be after him. It's a sad, awful story about your daddy, Horgan."

Horgan drops his hands through the air.

And Dutton settles into the depth of his voice. The wind moves over and between them and the birds face into it, ruffling feathers, letting the dust blow free. His voice is laden.

"So you know that it was such a far place away from here, and so long ago, that this all started. That was such a fine country back there, with slope everywhere, only parcels of flat ground along the creeks and rivers, and they were coveted, can you believe it. I mean your damn house sat on a hillside. You walked, and you walked up or down hill. Water run everywhere, and rain, rain, dew in the morning, fog of night, nary and never a crack in the ground. Those hills we grew up in, me and your dad, I think it's why he became so fine at ball; our center field was a little valley and you had to run uphill to catch a ball, left or right. I suppose you could have just waited on it, hunh?"

"Dutty."

"But that country and the country of the University were much alike, hills alike. The change of the country for us, from home to the college, wasn't that much. It was the change from there to here that was so extravagant. You need to remember this. Your daddy loved this country as ballfield, but that was all.''

"Well, then, why did he follow you?"

"I'm coming. So we went to the city and found the jobs at the University, working the grounds. We took care of the grass and trees. Your dad sent money home to his mother till she died. But he didn't play any pro ball. She had raised him all his life, and he was devoted, even though she wouldn't let him have the one thing he wanted. I'm a lesser person. I might've gone ahead and satisfied myself.

"But your father, he never even thought about anything but her. Sent her almost everything he had for seven or eight years. Didn't even go out at all, I mean even on dates with girls, because he thought his mother could put the money to better use. So we spent our ten years at college like a couple of monks, holed up in our dormitory room. It was a girls' college too. Girls by the hundreds around us. I did my share among them, but your father wasn't concerned with them. We mowed the grass, trimmed the trees and ivy, shoveled snow from sidewalks, day in and day out for the ten years. It was your father's great extravagance, every spring, to buy himself a new baseball. It wasn't that he wasn't interested; it was just that, and I think this is right, it was just that no one had ever made as strong of an impression upon him as his momma. And so when someone finally did, he became devoted to her too. This woman was your momma.

"But I'm not sure how much you know, how much he's told you."

"Dutty, all I know is I don't know that all this is any of my business," Horgan says. "When he talked about her I never listened."

"You just need to hear me. He wants you to know but can't bear, hasn't been able to bear, telling it himself. And now he can't so I'm here for him. You just tell me if I go over anything you are already acquainted with."

"Okay," Horgan says, nodding, nodding. He nods, listening, caught in the wind, staring at the rusted portions of the galvanized chain link.

"This woman that made the impression was your momma. She came three years after his momma died. That three years is the only part of his life I haven't seen him moving along without a burden, his devotion. But that's his concern. His devotions are and always have been his concern, his right. We've got no call over them, and I gave up long ago trying to talk him out of them. You won't try either, will you, Horgan? You've got to tell me that. That wouldn't be of any use at this stage. I found it and find it yet as incomprehensible, and maybe you will too, Horgan, but it's his business. In that we've got no right."

"It's not even reasonable," Horgan says, "to be devoted to someone he hasn't seen in almost forty years. He doesn't even know if she's dead or alive."

"Well. He knows that she was your mother."

"Oh, hell, Dutty. He was my mother," Horgan shouts.

"Horgan," Dutton says, and his voice is a pair of hands on Horgan's shoulders, pressing down. "Try to understand here. I've done it. You try it, son."

"God, Dutty, get on with what you're saying."

"Okay, okay. I've thought about it almost all of my life, for the past forty years. The impression was this: it was that she needed him and refused him at the same time. It was her pride, the audacity of it. It was his momma again, accepting his checks and devotion, telling him not to play ball. She was an abrupt girl, and he was a patient man.

"I met her first. Did you know that?"

Horgan shakes his head.

"I did. She was a student there at the college and I took her out several times before I caught up with how she was. I mean the way she was. The girls there at the school usually wouldn't even give us the time of day. They were mostly from better families, and I think we, as a group, the groundskeepers, were sort of a joke to them. And we were older, most of us. We were usually the butt of most of the school paper's cartoons and editorials. But she was different. I'd punch your daddy on the shoulder and nod when she walked by on campus. I finally noticed that she walked by more than most. Your daddy would look up, look at her, and then sort of half-smile at me, smile for my benefit. His lack of concern simply amazed me. She was a fine, good looking girl then. I couldn't tell if she was taking glances at me or your father. So I took advantage of your father's lack of interest and pursued her. I mean I actually got up off my knees, out of the flower bed, and followed her down the sidewalk.

"I caught up with her, but I wasn't the one she wanted. I mean we went out several times, but I wasn't the one she wanted. I was the type of what she wanted and so was your father: we were older. She was an intense young woman and on our outings she constantly discounted men her own age. She talked a great deal of her father. I found that she wasn't the one I wanted either, after a while, and so we parted company. It was a rather harsh parting, so

I was surprised to find, a bit later, she and your father together. I talked to him about her then, but he wouldn't listen. After only a few days he was devoted. I won't meddle with you, Horgan. I've always thought of her as a harsh and arrogant person. I was furious with your father for taking up with her. But he would just half-smile at me and say nothing.

"We had a ball game once. The staff of the college, and that included us as well as the faculty, played the local men's college ball team. It was a thing to get the two campuses together socially. Your father talked about it today. He remembered her up in the stands watching him pitch. He remembered her beauty. But I don't remember that at all. I remember her sitting in the stands with my Constance, who I'd met by then, and not watching your daddy, but absolutely abstaining from him, working on something completely different. I remember your dad throwing twenty-six strikeouts. The one ball hit went to first base, a little slow grounder. The president of the University stood there next to the bag, scooped it in, and stepped on the bag. I was playing second. You know what your dad did? He walked to first base and apologized to the president. She wasn't watching him. I absolutely know for a fact she wasn't.

"Then she was pregnant, and he was marrying her. I argued against it. I argued and argued with him but finally I gave up at it, disgusted with him. I was also with Constance then, falling in love with her, and I stayed with her to forget your daddy. He didn't act like he needed me, so I let it go."

"You argued against it? And her pregnant?" Horgan asks.

The old man stammers, "Yes. I did.

"So they married and all that time she was telling

him she'd take his name, but not his love. She didn't have time for that. She finished school, lived with your father for a few more months, had you, and went home. Left you with your father, and he took you gladly. But her leaving almost broke him. If he hadn't had you, it would have.

"Why she did it, Horgan, I know and I don't know. She went back for her father, for one. He'd raised her. But she had no concern for your father, or for you, leaving you both like that. I have always thought on it, and still don't understand it. Your father is yet devoted. He recalls her beauty, and the fact that she's your mother, and he is devoted.

"She wasn't watching your father on that ballfield. She was watching possibility. She found out she was pregnant, and your daddy was willing, so she took his name. She didn't tell her father. She wrote him letters telling him she'd have to stay in school an extra session. But she worked on your father all the same, trying to turn him into something she thought her father might accept. Your father didn't have any money, nor an education, so she asked him to do the one thing she knew he couldn't. She asked him to play ball.

"Your dad agonized over that.

"But when it came down to it, he couldn't. He was caught among his devotions. It was the first time I was ever glad he didn't play. I mean I'd been telling him he ought to play for years, but when she told him, I was against it.

"She left him and you, by the way I see it, because of two things.

"I have concentrated on this story so long it doesn't seem itself, like it's got no meaning at all.

"The first was that it was all something she hadn't

controlled, and couldn't control. She hadn't chosen, hadn't had her way. And then, even after she'd married, she couldn't have her way with your father. She got everything from him but the one thing she wanted most. She got more, and she got less. On this point she knew herself. I'll credit her that. She knew herself, especially by the time you were born. She wasn't at home with her body. Constance and I would go eat with her and your father after we'd married. All during the meal your mother talked of how she had no time for eating. For other things as well. She had no time for eating, or sleeping, or even sitting. She was constantly agitated, agitating. Something had always to be done. And the pregnancy got in the way of that. It would wear her out. She thought of it as being defeated in a way.

"But she might have stuck with it, I don't know, if it hadn't been for her father. She'd kept it all from him: the pregnancy, the marriage. Kept it from him, I suppose, because she was somehow afraid or ashamed. She said once that her father needed no one, had raised himself up to a fine stature by himself, had raised her too.

"But he found out, and he came east to see for himself, the same week you were born. I don't guess he believed it till he saw it himself. He was an old man then, she'd been born when he was old, and somehow it was as if it all breached him. I am not too familiar with him, but it was like it broke him in two, finding his daughter pregnant and married under those circumstances, behind his back, and so instead of taking it, he let it kill him. I didn't hear him speak three words that whole week. He got a hotel room and stayed there. Never saw or spoke to your father. Saw your mother only twice I think.

He died the same week you were born. His heart. Maybe it was all coincidence, his long trip east and being an old man, but she didn't take it that way. She saw it as connected, your birth and his death, and something about it horrified her. I guess she knew she was abrupt, but she never thought of herself as something less than her father thought her to be.

"She left when she was able, as soon as she was able to get out of the bed, left you with your dad, and took her father's body back home.

"Your father understood.

"I didn't. But I thought and still think it was the best thing for you. Maybe she knew that. I don't know. Maybe she knew herself.

"And your father remained devoted all through it. Till this day. That's his concern. She was beautiful, and perhaps there was some sweetness about her which she only let him see. No way to tell. But she couldn't have loved him, could she have? Or you. I don't see it. Maybe it was the best thing. But your father, still loving her till this day, because, because, she was devoted too, to something, needed and refused him, bore you, still loving her because he understands, at heart, something about her. But he has always been a man of great patience. His love never returned. I am amazed by his devotion.

"But even all this isn't the reason I'm here to tell. All this isn't what matters. What matters is the extent your dad's love went to and what we've kept from you."

Horgan pushes the hair out of his eyes, broaching his stillness, and the birds give a little hop on the backstop. "What, Dutty? I'm awful tired."

"It's that your dad has seen her since then. It

hasn't been thirty-nine years. And that I can tell you of her. I need to know if you want to know."

"Why," Horgan says, sitting up, and the birds taking wing, "wouldn't I be glad to know my birth?"

"After your birth, it wasn't your father that followed me here. It was me followed your father. I was worried for him.

"Your father, when we were kids and choosing sides for the ball game, he always picked me first even though I wasn't the best.

"He came here to be by her even though she did and still denies him. Horgan, your momma is Miss Eckley."

- 13 -

And Horgan thinks, no, I won't have it.

"He followed her here, a couple weeks after she left, and I came after him, to bring him away. He wouldn't have it. He just wouldn't have any part of it. He made some kind of deal with her—that he could stay as long as no one ever knew their relationship, including you. So she divorced him, and he signed the papers, started the ballfield. When I saw he wouldn't come back home with me I sent for Constance and we bought the farm with our savings.

"You know the rest. That's been forty years. She never has had anything to do with your father. He still basks in his unrequited love. But today was the first time I ever saw him feeling sorry for himself.

"Now, I don't know what you intend to do."

Well, I won't have it, he thinks.

"It's your affair now too. I don't think that she needs to know that you know. She might deny it completely. Who knows how her mind works. It is concerned, and always has been since she returned, with that elevator."

"I deny it too," Horgan says, stepping off the bleachers. He steps off the bleachers into the dirt, but he doesn't know what to do next. His mind is dry.

"I deny it too," he says again. "My dad would've told me."

"He didn't tell you because he knew, even though he loved her, that she wasn't good for you. But you're old enough now, Horgan, to take it and understand our fear. You're a man now."

Horgan opens his mouth, realizes he is about to say, "I am not a man," and stops. He backs up to the chain link, spreads his arms and catches his fingers in it, then slides down to the ground. His arms stretch out above him, taut. He tries to figure out why old Dutton would lie to him, why he would go to this extent to tell such a horrible lie in the middle of a hot day. And finding no motive, staring out through the burnt bleachers at the horizon, he tries to find some defect in his story. There must be hundreds of them. It was true, his father had never been interested in any woman as far as Horgan knew. Just his memory of Doris. Doris?

"Her name was Doris," Horgan says, looking up at Dutton, who sits on the bleachers, his hands folded. "My mom's name was Doris."

"We had to hide it from you. Your dad made up that name. We thought you might figure it out if you knew the name was Marian."

Horgan drops his head again. He makes crude circles in the dirt with his finger, concentrating on them, to forestall his thinking.

"How could anybody love anybody that much?" he says, not looking up.

"How much do you love Kidder?" Dutton asks. "I don't know. I hated giving up Constance when she died. I hated it worse than when my boy left. I don't know."

"How could anybody be as evil…"

"I don't know. Maybe she's not. She was honest about it from the first. Maybe God made her that way."

And before Horgan can move or say again, the CB on the fire truck cracks into the wind. He doesn't move, so Dutton says, "You've got a call, Horgan."

Horgan jumps, as if caught, and slams the chain link with both hands. "Goddammit," he screams, "goddamn, son of a bitch," and he runs for the truck, leaving Dutton standing there on the bleachers.

He jumps in, picks up the mike and answers. "Okay, this is Fire One, go ahead."

"Horgan, this is County MASH. We've looked all over for you. Could you come into the hospital now?"

"What? Why?"

"Your dad is in a bad way, Horgan. You need to come on in."

"I'm on my way," he says, and throws the mike toward the receiver. He jams the clutch and throttle down, almost breaks the key off in the ignition before the engine starts, and then winds the truck around the backstop, cutting across the blackened ballfield, circling old Dutton, to get back to the dirt road, and he is gone, standing on the pedal, holding the big wheel with both hands, watching the road ahead, and screaming down at the silent CB, "Tell him to wait, tell him to wait, goddammit."

He passes, yelling, a strung-out length of boys that is his ball team, passes them all on the dirt road, and the dust of his passing envelops them all. He enters the shadow of the elevator, slams over the Burlington-Northern tracks and there, not thinking he can see forever, to the very end of his life, but thinking he can't even see to the beginning, to the very start of his life. He has led his forty years on a false premise. In the beginning, he thinks, God snapped his fingers rhythmically. He kicks the brake and swerves out of the shadow onto the Route, and there he picks up speed.

Kidder cleans up the mess of feeding a Little League ball team. She rinses the plates and glasses and puts away the bread and lunch meat, walks around the house picking up potato chips and crusts of toast. She wipes the kitchen counters, drapes the rag over the sink, then goes into the living room. After the shades are drawn, and the room is cooler and darker, she rests in Horgan's armchair. She looks at the clock on the mantel, she slumps a bit, and folds her hands on her stomach.

He thinks there are too many things to think about. Don't think about anything. Wait. Wait to see what Dad says. He would've told. Why love her. Why love her.

He passes the firehouse, the La Motel, Whit's lumberyard, the Phillips 66, the Dairy Mart.

The Route shimmers and Horgan sees the white dashes and yellow center stripe rise from the road and hover a foot above it. The wind bleaches his face, tugging at his eyelids and lips, the looseness of his cheeks, and he can feel the back of his neck burnt. The chrome, plastic, and glass of his truck is too hot to touch, so he touches it anyway, cooling the steering wheel and gearshift knob with the first few layers of his skin, cauterizing his cat scratches.

What do I think.

My father waiting.

Dutton gathers the children under his arms.

He asks, "Do you boys know what to do?"

"Where's Coach gone?"

"He's on a call," Dutton says. "I'll help you boys practice."

"Coach told us what to do," Witherspoon says. "We know what to do."

"Okay."

And Dutton leads them into the back of his pickup. The boys climb in and then wait. Pillsneck walks in from afar, as they wait, and climbs in too. Dutton tells them all about the burnt ballfield then.

"It's burnt, but it's still flat," he says.

The boys, Dutton watches them, look at Pillsneck but don't say anything. They bow their heads, looking at their sneakers and mitts. The old man gets back in the cab of his truck with his grandson then and turns around on the dirt road, forward, reverse, forward, heading back toward the burnt ground.

Cat scratches. Cat scratches. Before. Before, the scratch on my cheek, and he reaches up, touching his cheek, and sees the burning house, the burning back room, before he stumbled and the cats scratched him, sees the clippings on the wall, curled and yellow, and they are all of him, clippings familiar, shapes he'd cut from the paper too, when he joined the service, pictures of the high school baseball team, when he got the fireman's job.

"Oh, God," he says, his mind aching, "oh, God," he says, "Daddy," and he pulls the fire engine into the parking lot of the hospital, barely able to turn the wheel, his arms weak, and when he stops, both feet pressing on the brake, the truck lurching and stopping, he leans on the big steering wheel and rests there, his chest hollow.

He rests there, taking deep breaths. He breathes,

thinking, my father is waiting. And when he thinks it the third time, he leans away from the wheel and climbs down out of the truck. He walks into the hospital out of the heat and brightness, shies instinctively from the smell of disinfectant and sickness. The old woman at the information desk is talking to him before he can make her out.

"They've moved him down to intensive care, Horgan," she says, and then he sees her pale arm pointing down a hallway.

He nods, something blue and patched still before his eyes, and follows her arm down the hallway to his father.

There is the memory of his father bending over him.

And, if she is my mother, why beleaguer me?

And, if she is my mother, why thwart me?

If she is my mother, why chastise me?

Even if she did not love my father, why not love me?

And how could he love her if she didn't love me?

Knowing him, how could he stand for it, her refusal to even acknowledge?

How could he stand to live here, knowing each day was a lie to me?

How could he, how can he, love her more than me?

There is the memory of his father, always bending over him.

He pushes through the heavy double doors of the intensive care unit, looking at the floor. He looks at the floor till someone speaks his name.

"Horgan?"

"Yes," he says, lifting his head.

The nurse says, "The doctor is with your father. He's in the third curtain down. Just pull it aside and go in."

"Thank you," he says, thinking, why do I have to walk so much?

He goes and pulls back the curtain, not looking where the bed and his father would be, but up at the rings of the curtain as they slide back along the rod. He does this so anything beyond the curtain will have time to notice him and adjust before he looks. He has always been embarrassed when someone else might be embarrassed, or called to account. So he takes his time watching the rings slide back, stepping in the enclosure, and pulling the curtain closed. When he finally turns around to look at his father and the doctor they still haven't noticed him. The doctor bends over his father, stethoscope to his sunken chest. His father sleeps.

And Horgan stands there for a minute, then is suddenly unable to wait a second longer, and he says, "Well?" Too loudly, he realizes, afterward.

The doctor jumps a bit, and another nurse pulls back the curtain behind him.

"I'm sorry," he says, turning, "I'm sorry."

The nurse pulls the curtain closed without replying.

Again he tells the doctor, "I'm sorry."

"He's had a bad time, Horgan. He got worse last night, but not much worse than he usually gets over that period of time. But I guess it's all accumulated, progressed to a stage where his heart and body are just too weak to cope with it. His heart skipped a bit this afternoon, and we brought him in here. I don't know what to tell you."

He speaks over his father's closed body. It stretches the length of the small bed but hardly raises the sheet above the mattress. The great long muscles of his arms fall away, melt away, from the bone, and his face, boiled and angular, is not his face. There is a thick, dried matter around both eyes.

"Can't we get this off of his eyes?" Horgan says, and he moves to the other side of the bed, rolling back the IV stand. He takes his father's head in his hands as he sleeps, pushing the thin hair back off his forehead, doing that twice, then wetting his finger and rubbing softly around the old man's eyes.

"Why doesn't he have his oxygen?" Horgan asks.

"He had us take it out this morning. You know how he hates it, and I don't know that it was doing him any good. It bothers him more than it helps, I think. You can wake him up, Horgan, if you'd like. He's had a little sleep."

"It won't hurt him? He don't hurt, does he?"

"There was a little pain when he had the attack, but that's all gone now. He'll be a little droopy-eyed. I'm going to go now. I'll come back in just a bit, and if you need anything ask one of the nurses. Okay?"

"Okay," Horgan says, and then catches the doctor as he's about to leave. "Thank you," he says, "I appreciate you being good to him these months."

"I'm very fond of him," he says, "He's a good man, Horgan. He's taken dying as well as anyone I've ever seen. As anyone who's seen it coming as long as he has. He's been a little bleary the past couple of days, but who wouldn't expect that."

And the doctor stops, looks at the old man, and says, "Well, I'll be back in a little while."

Horgan pulls the curtain to after he leaves.

My father waiting.

He pulls the sheet back up over his father's chest

and sits down to watch him breathe. He watches the gentle swell and fall of the spare sheet over his chest, and the pulse of the vein in his neck. Occasionally his eyes move behind the draped lids. And from his mouth the wind issues in soft, dry drafts that click as they come. His throat is tattered.

Horgan wets his finger with his tongue and rubs again the dry matter around his father's eyes.

"Dad," he says, whispering. Then louder, "Dad, it's me." And he takes his father by the ball and socket of his shoulder and rocks him a bit, "Dad."

And the old man cracks open like an egg, startled and the white of his eyes yellow and murky. He lies there for a moment, waking up, a splinter in his breathing, having to remember to breathe, mouth open, eyes up at the ceiling. When he settles, letting his head fall over toward Horgan, Horgan begins to breathe too.

"Dad," he says.

The old man pivots his hand and forearm up toward his face and signs, "Hello."

Horgan looks for a pad and pencil. "Would you rather have your paper and pencil, Dad?"

He moves his fingers slightly again. "No."

The long fingers fold then into a loose fist, resting. His veins run blue and thickly up, between, and over the bones of his forearm and wrist, matt in his hand under the mottled skin. The joints of his thumb and fingers seem knotted. They are purple and black, the movement of the bones bruising the flesh that holds them together. Horgan looks at his fingers and imagines he sees the indentations of a baseball's seams there.

"You haven't tried to talk today, have you?" Horgan asks.

His father dips his hand again.

"Are you hurting anywhere?"

The old man touches his lips and holds up three fingers. Horgan is so tired of the request he just shakes his head at first, then feels guilt and frustration for his inability and says what he's always said, what he has to say, "No, you can't have any water. Doctor said. Where's your sponge? I'll wet it for you."

His father reaches, without looking, to the small nightstand and gropes for the sponge. Horgan stands up and looks too.

"Here," he says, putting his father's arm back at his side on the bed. He gently lifts the old man's shoulder and takes the sponge from the crook of his neck where it has fallen. "You fell asleep with it."

Horgan takes the sponge out into the open area of the unit, wets it in a sink, and walks back to his father. He takes his time. I am taking my father's time, he thinks. He sits down again, and dabs at his father's dry lips.

"You're getting all the water you need through that IV," he says.

He dabs at the corners of his mouth, pressing every drop out of the sponge he can.

"It's true, all that stuff, Dad?" he asks, quietly, looking at the sponge, glancing up at his father's eyes, looking at the sponge. "All that stuff Dutton said?"

His father lifts his hand into the air and signs, "What did say?"

"About Miss Eckley and you. About her being my mother."

His father drops his hand, raises it up again. He makes a loose fist, his thumb up between the index and middle finger, then lifting the middle and index fingers, crosses them, then holds them together and tilted a bit, then lets all four fingertips drop to the nail and back of his thumb.

"True."

Horgan recognizes the letters but doesn't hold them, holds instead the grace yet of his father's hand so close to death. His hand revolves, flutters, and stalls—bone, vein, blood, and leather—rises and drifts, falling, like a bird. With a wind beneath him. His father is a pitch. His father is a game of catch. Horgan dives in a plowed field for a ball. His father settles his cap on his head, tilted back. Horgan watches his hand spell again.

"I was going to tell you."

"For Christ's sake, when? You're dying," Horgan says, running, running to be under the ball's fall in a night game, whispering Father, Father, Father, Father, hoping for a lucky catch, a miracle, but losing it in the stars, among all those suns.

His father drops his hand, his hand signing falling, signing, "No, no..." to the white sheet.

Horgan is still running when he hears the shrill of his father. He looks up from his lap and sees his father's mouth almost closed, the parched lips trembling and the sound coming from where it's not supposed to. It comes quietly but in a high pitch like a mouse burning.

"Don't," Horgan says, standing up, then sitting back down slowly and touching his father's temple with the palm of his hand, "Don't cry, Dad, I'm sorry, don't cry, you'll hurt something, I'm sorry."

Ooper lies on his back a hundred yards down the hushed stream, in the sanctity of the ditch, where water has once been. He gazes up past his swelling cheek into the grass bordered sky and makes preparation. The dirt that he lifts up and casts over himself, over his bruised cheek, over his fine green suit, is from the floor of the ditch and is very fine. If it had the means it would be silt, but as it is, it's simply more dust, more of the same. Dust's means, the wind, carry it, floating, the length of his body and then up, up above the table of the land where it is a small red puff, and then it dissipates. A handful of dust here doesn't last; it doesn't go far. Ooper casts and casts. He covers himself casting, all but the sockets of his eyes, his flaring nostrils, the tips of his shoes, and his bow tie, which is silk. The dirt slides off of it. He lies as still as possible then. Even when a bird flutters across above, then returns to the bank of the ditch on foot and peeks over the edge at him, he doesn't move.

And sitting there over his father, knowing the tale for truth, and believing it, still appalled by it, but believing it, believing it as much as if he were any character in a book and these events happened to him, and seeing it from that distance, he suddenly realizes the story's complete insignificance to his present life. He has found that his father was strangely, terribly devoted—that his long gone mother, who he had never known and consequently never personally missed, was alive—that she was a woman he didn't care for, a woman that had even tried, occasionally, to thwart the even running of his life. He would wake up with Kidder on Monday morning, put his blue shirt on like always.

"It doesn't matter," Horgan says, looking for a way out of his silence, looking for a way to quell his father.

His father lifts his hand, "What?"

"All that Dutton said. It doesn't matter."

His father visibly starts. Horgan reaches down and puts his hands on his shoulders. He is about to yell for the nurse when his father throws his brisk hand into the air. Horgan takes the hand in both of his and says, "Slow down. I can't read it that fast."

"Dutton says what else?" his father signs to him.

"All that I told you, Dad, nothing else. What else is there?"

"Nothing," his father signs. "Asleep with my eyes open."

"You need to rest, Dad. Everything's okay," Horgan says.

And his father signs, "No."

And his asking, his admission, is said in the way of an apology.

Horgan burns with it.

His father signs, "Maybe she'll come."

He burns and burns with it, seeing himself before the woman, like his father at one time, asking for his father. His father suggests, asks, then lowers his gaze, drops his hand slowly.

Horgan folds both of his hands in his lap, folds them into fists. "Don't you know her by now?" he seethes. "Don't you understand her by now?" He drives the questions into his father. He feels, sitting there with his fists and rage, so much shame for his father, boiling over the sorrow, that he says it knowing he shouldn't, "That woman is the devil's bitch."

His father lifts the hand closest to Horgan, the hand with the IV needle running up a vein in the back, and backhands Horgan weakly across the cheek.

Horgan grabs his father's wrist and holds the hand in midair, captured. He adjusts the needle, back to its proper position, and his father winces. Then he puts the hand back on the bed.

His father's eyes are glazed and running. The old man raises the far hand and signs, "I wouldn't say ever against sweet Kidder."

And Horgan, mixed, captured, enough of his own shame now. There. Kidder and Miss Eckley in the same thought. Something unbearably ugly. No.

Akton searches Ooper's tent and then drives slowly through the streets of Eckley in his patrol car. He pulls behind the Phillips 66 and the Dairy Mart, checking behind the dumpsters, then stops at Whit's lumberyard and walks among the stacks of lumber and shingles. He puts his hands on his hips many times, looking around. When he crosses the railroad tracks on his way back to the elevator he stops and gets out of the car, walks back to the culvert running under the road. He jumps down in the ditch, after kicking at the tall weeds for snakes, and bends down to peer through the long, hollow corrugated tube.

The boys see the bus almost a full half-mile away, as it crests the tracks. They come off the black field in twos and threes, but silently, to the cover of old man Dutton and their home dugout.

"What are we gonna do?" one of the Rutley twins asks.

Witherspoon tries to work up a spit, but is unable and has to say "Hunh!" in disdain, instead.

"Where's Coach?" Whit asks.

"My arm feels funny," Gaspar throws in.

"Now, boys, boys," Dutton suggests.

Yanks says, "Well, let's be hitters, fellas," and he takes a can't miss, sure swing at the air.

The bus rolls up, brakes squealing, to the visitors' dugout. It is a long green bus printed with the words "SPRINGTOWN ROCK OF JESUS CHURCH" in large white block letters, and, in a slightly smaller script, "Army Cooper, Pastor." Springtown is the only town for hundreds of miles that isn't named for its elevator. It is named for the only spring within hundreds of miles. The bus is full of people. The first man off, a man all belly, chin, forehead, baseball cap, and cigar, stops in mid-step, one foot on the ground and one still in the bus, like the first man on the moon, and shouts, "My God, they've tried to burn us out," and then, that not enough, adds, "And look, somebody's took the lid off this country." Only then does he let anyone else off the bus. The Springtown ball team thumps out, each boy over five feet as it appears from the home dugout, and then their assorted parents, grandparents, brothers, sisters, and hangers-on, ninety-five of them altogether. They run, skip, and meander to the home team's dugout and stand outside of it there, whispering to each other, exchanging grins and sticking their fingers through the chain link at Horgan's boys. The boys flutter and flit about the dugout and at last flock to Dutton's protecting arms.

"I'm sorry, Dad. Please, don't hit me no more," Horgan says.

His father signs, his hand reaching up out of a well, "Don't turn your mind against your mother. Leave her to heaven."

"But why her?" Horgan asks. "What was there in her? She isn't like Kidder at all. Not at all."

"You don't know what it was," his father signs, tiring, his hand slowly and slower. "She was something different then, before her father died."

"But since then," Horgan says, still unable not to push, "since then, why? As far as I've known she's never paid any attention to you or me. She fought us over the fireman's job. She pushed me into quitting out at the elevator. Just three days ago she slammed her door in my face after I told her my life wasn't any of... her business.''

His father looks up.

"She wanted me to stop drinking beer at the ball games," Horgan explains.

"You probably shouldn't. I agree with her," his father signs.

"Oh, my God," Horgan shouts, and stands up, before his father is through with the phrase. "My Lord," he says. "And the reason she tried to get the Fire Department abolished was because she didn't want me taking dangerous work right? And when I went to work out at the elevator she pushed me twice as hard as anyone else because I was her son and some day she meant to turn the business over to me? Dad, it's too late for that. I can't reinterpret her life to fit your conscience. What I want to know is why, why since then have you remained," and the word doesn't want to come out; it embarrasses him, and angers him still, to say it, "devoted? Why?"

And his father signs, for hours it seems to Horgan, signing with care and respect, but slowly and slower, like the last of a wind. And not starting his explanation with the word "Marian," or even "Doris," but with "Miss Eckley." "Miss Eckley," he signs, his hand in the sky, Horgan thinking, this gentle sorry man, "is the hard line the world must take sometimes in order to survive. We couldn't make it, you and I, without her. And she's your momma. She couldn't be expected to handle both jobs. I took you gladly.''

Finally, half an hour before game time, the mothers begin to arrive. The mothers of Eckley. The mother of Sickopoose pulls up in a battered farm truck, the red dust of her line drive training still between her toes. She knocks three people off the fence of the dugout while carrying a cooler to the boys.

"What'd you bring this week, Mrs. Sickopoose?" Whit asks. He has his glove held behind his back.

"Lime, Whit," she says, smiling. Then she slams the lid of the cooler against the chain link to back a few more Springtown gawkers off.

Shrugsby watches Mrs. Yanks slam the door to her station wagon and stride toward the dugout, her purse swinging wildly, careening off her hip. He nudges Yanks in the ribs and nods toward his oncoming mother. "I forgot," Shrugsby says. "I forgot to tell you. Your momma said she was going to bust your butt for leaving the house this morning."

Yanks stands up. "Why me?" he says. "Why's she going to spank me?"

"'Cause you're nine and ought to know better," Shrugsby says, and he leans back against the chain link and crosses one leg over the other. Then he adds, "She probably loves you too. You ought to be ashamed for running away from home like that."

Yanks is about to argue with him when his mother pulls him out of the dugout through the maze of boys and into the open area in front of the bleachers.

She holds him by the wrist as he orbits her, a step ahead of her open palm. "I'm 'shamed, Momma!" he screams, "I'm 'shamed!"

Horgan turns, looking at everything within the curtain but his father. He exhausts the monitors of the equipment, the slow dropping of the IV bottles, the convolutions of the tubing, the wafting of the curtains when a nurse passes by beyond. Hard line is right, he thinks. I never expected anything, he thinks. Finally, he turns back to his father and his father's arm almost jumps at him.

"Your face?" the old man signs.

Horgan touches his face. The scratches. He decides abruptly, without hesitation, not to tell. Deciding it would be best for him.

"A cat did that," he says. "There was a fire at the ballfield and a cat scratched me."

His father holds motionless his hand in midair. Then he signs slowly, as if he's not sure, "Game yesterday?"

"No. Today. It's this evening."

"When?" he signs.

Horgan looks at his watch. "Half an hour," he says.

"Go now," he signs.

"No, I'm going to stay here with you. The boys know what to do."

"Go now." His father, after signing, slams as best he can the mattress with his open palm.

"Dad, you're sick and I'm staying. You're crazy if you think I'm going to a ball game."

"You'll let boys down," his father signs. "It's your responsibility."

"It was hers too," Horgan says, and he stares at his father.

His father turns away for a moment, letting his cheek fall to the pillow. It is a great effort that enables him to turn back. The tendons pull taut in his lagging throat.

"Go now," he signs.

And Horgan lifts his own hand, and lifting further, lifts his middle finger, signing to his father. "No," he says, behind his hand.

The old man frowns. "Go. Don't wait on me.

Please. We've had all this time. I want to sleep. Win for me.'' And his father refuses to acknowledge anything else Horgan says or does. He lets his head fall to the pillow again, sink into it, and his lids roll over the low place of his eyes.

Horgan gets up and calls the nurse.

"He's asleep," she says. "He's just asleep."

And Horgan says, "Okay."

He watches the nurse leave and sits back down and then watches his father sleeping. There is little change. He does not get better. Horgan rubs the old man's long, slack arm.

"I'm going now," he says to his father. "I'm going. You'll be better."

He gets up again, letting his fingertips slide along his father's abdomen, hip, and leg, holding his foot for a moment, and then dips out the curtain, thanks the nurse, walks back down the hallway thinking, loving that which won't have you, which thwarts you, which asks of you what you cannot do. Asking you to be what you are unable to be.

"How is he, Horgan?" the old lady with the pointing arm asks.

"He's asleep now, Mearl. Can I use your phone? I want to have Kidder come down and stay with him for a while."

"Sure, Horgan."

She watches him dial with her mouth closed.

"I shouldn't leave him now, Mearl, but I've got the ball game."

"You've been here all this time, Horgan, honey. You've been a good boy."

"He wants me to go," Horgan explains.

"Then you should."

"Hello?" Kidder says.

"Hi honey, it's me. I'm down here at the hospital. Can you come?"

"I was just about to walk out the door for my appointment. What's wrong?"

"Daddy's real bad."

"I'm coming right now, Horgan."

"Okay. But I won't be here. Go ahead and go to your appointment first. He's asleep, I think, right now. Then go stay with him. He's in the intensive care unit."

"Where will you be?"

"I'm going to the ball game. I'll be back at the hospital as soon as it's over. So don't leave him till I get back, okay?"

"Why are you going to the game?"

"He wants me to."

"Okay," she says, "I'll be with him when you get there."

"Bye," he says, "I love you."

"I'll be with him, honey. I love you too. Bye bye."

And Horgan hands the phone back to the receptionist.

He says, "Thank you."

And she says, "You're welcome, Horgan. Bye bye."

And he, already on his way, his mind working in three different directions, says, "Bye, honey," and kicks open the hospital door. And outside in the parking lot, the weather of his world trying to blow him out, he concentrates on the drive to the ballfield, along the Route, past the elevator and down the dirt road, which he knows he will not be able to make without a further crushing of the splintered bones of birds.

- 14 -

It is the middle of the night and he is up and hungry but doesn't know what he wants. He actually aches with his hunger and his unknowing, his inability to find something to feed it. This is what it is like. Raging at the solid. It is like screaming at the heat, or darkness, or the past. She is my mother. It is not fair to be given a mother forty years after the fact. I would rather not have one, he thinks. I would rather think of Kidder. I would rather think of my father alone. I am not selfish.

What was wrong with him? There is nothing wrong with him. Why not love him?

He is thirty-thousand feet above Eckley, lying in the tail of a KC-135, and a jet fighter swoops in under him in a long swift arc. It takes the jet only seconds to come from the perfect empty blueness and fill up Horgan's life. Horgan dumps fuel into the plane's tanks, and the jet flares away, up, and far ahead, as if Horgan is standing still. It hurts his eyes, the plane moves so quickly to somewhere else. He looks back down at the earth, and from this height, he does not move. The points don't change. He lifts back up, places his chin in the rest strap, and he looks back at the place he has supposedly been, more of the same color, that open blue, and he waits for something else to catch up with him.

Don't wait on me.

Why wait on her?

And later, he steps back out on the open platform and stands there all day. The connections of the rails thump by rhythmically under, marking units of time. He rides west in his caboose and the sun rises between the rails like an "aha!" and follows him, staring at his incredulity all day as it rises and follows, and finally passes him, overhead. And goes on beyond. He is almost ashamed to be going the same direction.

There, there, Horgan, he thinks, if the Fire Department had two men you'd probably ride on the back of the truck. There you'd feel at home.

And earlier, the ball starting at home plate and his vision unable to pick up on it quickly enough, the ball coming straight at him, and he turning but far too late and it rails overhead and beyond him, hits the hard ground, and rolls forever away from him on the flatness, his back and butt chugging away for the bleachers and the ball teams, running out into the emptiness for a round thing he uncontrollably loved.

The day as it moves toward evening, the long afternoon and the heat inconceivably building still.

I don't want her but my father does. Using this as reason and excuse.

And pulling into the gravel lot of the elevator and shutting down the engine, he thinks, she could have, at the least, let me understand why I couldn't play ball, that I got her height and coordination instead of his. And he steps down, lightly, to the brittle earth. He looks off to the ballfield in the distance and sees the green block of the Springtown bus and the rows of glinting automobiles, the tiny specks of boys in the field. And he thinks, somehow relieved, that he will not have much time for her. He can do what he can do and that's all. There are his boys waiting. His father was right. He glimpses an opening in the boys.

Horgan turns back toward the elevator and his eyes fill with dust. He bows his head, rubs his eyes, and bends into the choked wind toward the elevator.

The birds sit in a line along the railings and ridge-rows of the train cars, perch on the edges of the chutes and hoppers, and high up above the bins they circle. They look for an opportunity to glide and stall to the ground, to the concrete platform, or down between the rails of the Burlington-Northern, and feed, where they hop from grain to grain, grain to pellet, looking up between each careful peck. Horgan comes upon them and shoos them purposely. They rise and perch, then fall again as he passes.

He crosses between the buckling cars again, more carefully, and pulls himself up on the platform. The dust is thicker now than earlier in the day. Chaff and seed are deep on the platform; they blow and drift against the tin. All of the men move about in masks that look like safety cups. The masks are the color of the dust, the same color as each man's face. The men work mutely, signing to each other through the noise and chaff.

Miss Eckley's tin door still has Gaspar's mark, the round dent of his strike. Horgan clenches his fist, lifts it, and pounds on the door above the dent. His knocking echoes against the tin walls of her office and resounds in his skull. His pounding satisfies him.

It's Akton that opens the door. He opens it, looking down at Horgan, and slowly steps back, dragging the door with him. Its swinging reveals Miss Eckley, sitting behind her desk.

He notices first her arms, spread on the desk. They are his arms. The tapered wrist, the small hand, the short muscle. It weakens and enrages him; he falters and steps forward.

"What?" she says, "What in the hell do you want now?"

My God, how could he have not known? His eyes, the line of his jaw, his small, even teeth, and the widow's peak. She stands up behind the desk, as sharp as a piece of tin blown across a field. Horgan reaches up and touches his own face.

"The dust," he says, "it's worse. You need to shut down."

"I don't need you here. Get off my property."

"You don't need anybody, do you?" Horgan says, and immediately feels Akton looming. He turns his way and says, "You don't need plumbers. You just have water brought in." This stops Akton for a moment. Akton turns, stupidly, Horgan thinks, to Miss Eckley, for direction. Drum your lips with your fingers now, you idiot, you loaf of bread. "You haven't moved a stick of furniture in your house in the last forty years. It was too heavy, wasn't it? And all those bent nails around your boarded up windows. That shack falling into such rot that it needed burning. And now you're going to blow this town to kingdom come."

"Deputy," she orders, "get this man off of my property."

Akton steps toward him.

"Wait," Horgan says, "God knows I have. The

least spark will set this dust off. I can't imagine what it must be like inside one of those bins. The least you can do is let the men who want to leave do that."

Miss Eckley just stands there, her lips drawn tightly closed, her eyes slits. It angers Horgan. He waits a moment longer.

"You can't just kill men like birds," he shouts.

"Get him out of here," the old woman screams.

And Akton steps forward and puts Horgan in an arm lock, then slides around behind him and picks him wholly off the ground. Horgan tries to tear his arms loose but can't get free. He flails with his forearms and hands and swings his legs back, kicking at Akton as he carries him out the door and starts across the platform. There is nothing he can do to get free. His chest begins to hurt. In desperation he grabs hold of Akton's belt and yanks up hard.

"Goddammit! You son of a bitch!" Akton belches, and turns momentarily to one side to get to Horgan's grip.

When he turns Horgan sees her at the tin door. She is closing it. She watches, calmly, Akton handle him, and Horgan, seeing her face in calm, is suddenly pierced with self-pity, and the emotion sickens and enrages him. He screams.

He screams, "Mother!" And screams it again, "Mother!" Crying out at her. And dipping in Akton's arms his eye meets Akton's knee and then he is dropped to the concrete. And it is on the way back up to meet Akton's fist that he hears her telling him to stop.

She says, "Let him be."

Horgan watches her calves and feet move out toward him. His eye leaks on the platform.

"Let him be," she says again, and Akton drops him back to the concrete.

"He was cursing you," Akton says. "I heard him."

"Get out of here," she says. "Go on. I'll handle him."

"Hell," Akton says.

She faces him, standing over Horgan. "You're worthless. Get out of here."

"Goddamn pleased," Akton says, and he turns and walks off.

Miss Eckley watches him off the platform and then turns away herself, back toward her office. A group of men stand around Horgan, and one of them helps him up after Miss Eckley shuts her door. Horgan tucks in his shirt, then looks up at the men.

"This place is dangerous," he tells them. Horgan is serious, but some of the men laugh. "There's too much dust. You all know that. You ought to go on away from here." And he walks back to the marked door.

Walks back and stands there in front of it, deciding whether he should knock or not, deciding whether he's now still bound to knock, or, since she now knows, is now reminded that he is her son, perhaps he can just skip the formality and walk on in, yell, "I'm home, Mom," with his hand in the cookie jar. He turns his head, looking around. The group of men still stand there, watching him. He looks up, and a line of birds on the edge of the tin roof curl their necks to look at him. He opens the door and steps in, closing it without looking up in the manner of his father's curtain.

And there is no softness about her, unless it is her hands hidden beneath the desk. She is as sharp as a splintered bone. She sits at the steel desk, beneath the three engravings, and says nothing. Looks up at him, but doesn't say a word.

I have her, Horgan thinks. She's old and her time has come. He moves to the chair Akton had been sitting in and sits down. He crosses one leg over the other and breathes heavily for a few moments. He's been holding his breath since the fight.

She turns to him when the squeaking of his chair permits, quits, and she says, "So you know. You were not to know. Would God you'd never found out."

She brings her hands out from beneath the desk to say these things, and through, she hides them again. She reaches back up and pulls an invoice under her stare.

What is she thinking? Horgan rubs at the fine rings of black dirt on his neck: ash off his ballfield and bleachers. The sun itself must be outside the door of the little tin office. Sweat runs off Miss Eckley's face and occasionally she will reveal her hand to push her sparse white hair back up off her forehead. What can she be thinking? Maybe it will kill her. Horgan watches while something strikes her.

She pushes the invoice away and says, "Your father reneged on our agreement. It's typical of him."

"My father will probably die tonight." He says this calmly, astounding himself. He says it for her reaction, but the saying of it backfires, and he feels lost again, suddenly dropped into the desert. He thinks he will never be quenched again. He wants to take it back.

Her reaction: to move a sheet of onionskin paper and watch the dust lift from its movement.

It angers him after a bit, her watching the motes

fall back, and he says, "There's nothing typical about him. It's your kind that's typical."

"I don't have to speak to you," she says. "We have no acquaintance other than that first occasion. I had little part in you. Your father comes to this town like some kind of..."

"Shut up," Horgan yells, and he rises to his feet, but doesn't step forward. "Just shut up."

She halts for a moment, giving him the moment, but goes on, "Comes to this place and begins, of all things, a nursery. Have you seen a tree start here? Have you seen any growing thing start here? He had an opportunity and wasted it. He would rather be mayor of this place. Mayor of this place. It is typical of him to wait this long to tell you. He hadn't the courage. He hadn't the grasp. He hadn't the ner..."

"He didn't have the heart," Horgan says. "He didn't have the heart to reveal you to me. And there was your agreement too, wasn't there? Where is that piece of paper filed away? Did it burn today? Did it burn today?" he asks.

"I don't have to speak to you," she yells back at him. "I'm not bound to that at all. I have work to do."

When she yells, Horgan sits back down. This is not what he needs, wants. He needs to calm her.

"You shouldn't have found out, that's all," Miss Eckley says, and she moves her chair back against the tin wall. "You shouldn't have found out. That was the agreement."

"It was Dutton that told me," Horgan says, trying to soften her toward his father. "Look," he says, and he holds his open, gesturing hand by the wrist with his other hand, "Look, I don't want anything. I'm sorry about your house. I just want one thing."

She begins to shake her head and says, "This knowledge will make no difference in how I run this elevator. I won't shut down."

"No, no," Horgan says, "To hell with the elevator. You can blow up the whole planet for all I care. But I want you to go see my father."

She does not look at him, so he says, "Please."

"No."

"Why not?"

"I haven't the time."

"It's him that's not got the time," Horgan says, his voice caught between two levels, rising.

"I won't," she says.

"Look, if you haven't got any compassion, at least assume the virtue. He's dying. All he seems to have is your memory. I don't know why. But please."

"I never loved him. I gave him you. I told him then, and he understood, that that would be all he'd get."

"Damn you!" Horgan screams, rising, "damn you, damn you, damn you!" And he stalks the front of her desk, holding his fists to his sides. And then again, still not accepting her, "Damn you, woman. Damn you. This was your husband..."

"No," Miss Eckley shouts, rising too, behind the desk, "No, he wasn't!"

Horgan stops.

"No, he wasn't," she says again, her palms flat to the desk top. "He is not my responsibility."

"A divorce doesn't mean the marriage didn't take place," Horgan shouts.

"I didn't get a divorce," she says, "That marriage was annulled. It didn't happen."

"What?"

"It was annulled."

"You were with him for almost a year. You can't annul a marriage after a year," Horgan says. "He was your husband. You can't deny that."

"It was annulled. I do deny it, and I did then."

"Look," Horgan says, "You can't annul a marriage after that much time."

"You can if it hasn't been consummated," she says.

"What?" Horgan screams, almost laughing. "What? You can't deny me too, lady. What about me? You can't annul me."

She pauses for a moment, her shoulders forming curves. And then something rises in her again. "No," she says, "that Dutton won't leave me with this. He and your father can't do this to me. They haven't given me my due. They can't leave this with me. You go back to them. That thing was annulled. It was never consummated. Your father provided a name." And she pauses. "I was taken forcibly long before I met him."

"What?"

"I was taken forcibly before your father. We stayed together but it was for appearance."

"You were raped?" Horgan asks.

"I was taken forcibly."

"My father raped you?"

"No," she says, slamming the desk top with her fist.

"Who then?"

"I don't know. It was dark and I don't know. It was dark, and he was covered."

And Horgan, dropping to the concrete floor of the office and sitting there, eyes open but not seeing, understanding immediately that he was made and not born.

Miss Eckley is my mother but my father raised and made me. I love baseball but cannot play. My virgin father. Why Dutton argued against it. Not so much that they've hidden my mother all these years as they have been hiding my father. I am not my father's son.

Miss Eckley stands up on tiptoe, looking over the desk at Horgan. "They weren't giving me my due," she says softly. Her shoulders are curved again and there is a dearth of slack skin hanging from her elbows.

"I never had a goddamn chance," Horgan whispers. He looks up at her, his hands spread over his raised knees. "Somebody should have told me why I couldn't play ball. I was just a kid." He is nine, out in a flat space, tossing a ball and hitting it up, a pop fly, and then dropping the bat and running to catch it in his bare hands; throwing the ball up on the roof, listening for its tin smack and furrowed roll, its bouncing over the leadhead nails, and then raising his glove at the last moment to pocket its fall; out in the red dust of a plowed field learning to dive, again and again the dirt in his eyes; sliding into anything, pitching and throwing, swinging, running from sack to sack; pointless, useless, impossible.

"You weren't his son," she says, looking down at him still.

"I am too," Horgan says, "I'm every bit his son. I'm none of yours."

"What?"

"I'm none of yours. He saved your ass, didn't he? Dutton wouldn't, but my father did. But it was only for a while. Till your father wouldn't accept excuses any longer. Till he put this elevator on hold for a week and went to get you. Did he believe you were raped or did you just not tell him? But that wasn't what really mattered. What mattered, right, was that he was your father, and you hid your life from him. That's what killed him, right? The hiding from him. Like he was a kind of beast.''

"It's none of your business," she says.

"It is, it is. He was my grandpa."

"You killed him," she spits. "It was you that killed him. You." And she holds her arm out, pointing at him.

"Then for Christ's sake," Horgan pleads, "why didn't you just kill me when you had the chance?"

She sits back down. She hides her hands. "It was different then. I was different then. And after a while I'd found your father and we'd made our agreement. I thought I'd get away with it. You don't know how it was."

"I didn't kill him," Horgan says, and a moment later he adds, "And you didn't either. People get old and they die. If it's their busted sense of ethics that kills them that's just another form of dying of old age."

"I don't have time for this," Miss Eckley says.

"You haven't had time for anything since then," he follows. "Except shuffling grain from one bucket to another."

"And you? And you?" she curses, "Respite and danger, respite and danger. Never any productive work. Your life wasted on baseball and waiting on an adventure."

"Go to hell," he says, "you don't know anything about my life, Mother, clippings or not. You don't have any idea of me. You can't give me away and then challenge my life too. You haven't got any right. You haven't got the least right. You've got no stinking right. Wasted? Why? Because I wouldn't poison birds for you? I am my father's son. Do you hear me? I'm my dad's son." He says this in the way of a threat, threatening her and backing out the tin door. "I haven't waited for anything," he screams back at her from the platform.

She stands in the doorway to her office. She steps out, arms spread, and yells back at him, "Look on this. Look on my work."

"Hug your goddamn elevator," Horgan yells. "Hug it till it explodes."

And she screams over his noise and the louder noise of the elevator itself, "I don't have the patience for you. I never had the patience for you. I did what was right, so damn you and me both."

The men on the platform have all stopped and now watch them. They look between Horgan and Miss Eckley.

Horgan backs up to the edge of the platform and realizes he's blown his chances. He stands there, staring at her, she with her hands upon her hips, and he tries, trying not to, tries to imagine her with her belly full. He jumps down to the gravel bed of the Burlington-Northern and turns back to her. Only his shoulders and head are visible above the concrete.

"He loves you," he screams back at her. "He's an old man," he says. And he says, "Please," before he finally turns, running toward his fire engine.

- 15 -

In the dog's blanched afternoon of the day, Horgan rolls slowly down the dirt road toward the ballfield. The home bleachers stand when they see his big red fire truck approach, the huge curl of its dust rising behind.

Kidder, Horgan thinks, please, Kidder. I need.

Whit climbs the chain link fence of the dugout and yells, "It's Coach!"

I have been left out so long not knowing I was left out. I have been waiting for something that's already occurred.

Dutton waves the boys back off the field. The game is about to start, but Dutton waves them in. The Springtown batter backs out of the box and the umpire raises up, places his hands on his hips.

"What the hell?" the far coach cries. He marches out of his dugout, pulling the cigar from the stomach of his face. His jaw unhinges and his mouth drops open in appalled disgust. His expression says, "Call the game, get back on the bus, boys, we won't be a part of murdering baby rabbits." He holds his arms out, lifting his shirt so that his belly, cleaved by his belt, shows in a pearly pout. He yells, "Are we gonna play or not?" and in forlorn desperation turns once to the umpire and once to the crowd behind him. "I brought these boys to play."

Kidder. I am a man who pities himself occasionally. So your father is not your father. Your father is a dark other. And your mother is not Doris, but Miss Eckley, and Doris too. And the difference this makes is... Kidder. Here is a woman who has a child, is able, and does not refuse it but gives and neglects it. And I am full of desire and am unable. In my unable love. A one without patience. Here me patient; I am a patient man who pities himself occasionally, who is only impatient with his past.

The day is on the edge of burning, burning not just the parched brush, the earth, its slow creatures, but the day itself about to smoke and burst, turn black.

Miss Eckley's cats have all been treed by the dogs of Eckley.

He climbs down from the truck slowly, watching his boys run off the field, and tries not to allow himself any more room than the game to think.

But I have always been patient with the present moment. I have even liked it.

He walks across the red banded black ground and into his chanting dugout. Dutton puts his hand on Horgan's shoulder, and Horgan smiles at him, walking on through.

"Sit down, boys," Horgan says, and he moves out onto the field to meet the Springtown coach.

"We got a game today or not?" the coach asks, raising his eyebrows into the vast furrowed plain of bewilderment.

The lady who helped Horgan with the tight cap on his fireplug rises from her seat behind home plate and screams, "Knife him, Horgan!"

Horgan says, "Give me a couple minutes, Coach. And we'll be right out. I appreciate it."

"Have you got another field? This one's burnt."

"It's the only one we've got," Horgan says, and he turns back to the dugout. You toilet brush, he thinks, you drip bucket.

The far coach raises his arms again, encompassing all known religions.

Perhaps it was true. Perhaps he'd waited too long. But he hadn't had Kidder. It was something that time had worked on him.

He takes his lineup clipboard from Dutton and the old man says, "He's a fat one, isn't he, Horgan?"

"He's the fattest," Horgan says.

The boys are lined up along the fence inside the dugout, their noses and fingers hanging through the chain link. On the way back in Horgan runs the base of his clipboard along the line of their fingers and they yip in turn.

"Get them minkers back inside," he says. "You'll lose one to a foul ball one of these days."

The boys back up to the bench and sit down and Horgan kneels in front of them in the red dirt. There is the smell of their washed shirts, the sweat of the headbands in their caps, and the leather of their gloves. It smells to him of home. The wind blows through the chain link, under and over the tilted, twisted, and gnarled brims of their caps, and directly into his eyes. The water starts from them easily. But before he can say a word Pillsneck's father climbs down out of the bleachers and stands behind the fence of the dugout.

"Yes?" Horgan says.

Pillsneck's father is Pillsneck times three. He says,

"My boy is your best pitcher. He should pitch today. You're not much of a coach if you can't see that."

Horgan does not rise. And he does not bother to explain. He decides he would just as soon fight this man as talk to him. He says, "Please, sir, don't speak of my socks. It's an old story, full of anguish and pride, tears and black eyes, old loves, a dead man, a supreme consummation, and a faded dream."

Witherspoon asks, "What happened to your eye, Coach?"

He'd felt the swelling but hadn't touched the spot yet. He looks up at Pillsneck's father and does so, smiling.

Pillsneck's father grimaces, says, "You think about what I said," and backs away.

Horgan yells, "I will! I will!" and he watches him back away and sit on the second step of the bleachers. Witherspoon's great uncles, the old turtles, get up from their places and sit on either side of him.

"You go pitch 'em a game, little Gaspar!" Gaspar's mother yells. "Us parents will just sit here in the bleachers where we belong from now on." And she glares in someone's direction.

Horgan whispers to his boys. "Did you get that new glove broke in, Feeb?"

"It's just like my granny's throat, Coach," Feeb says, and he claps the maw of his black glove open and shut.

"Find an old mattress, Gasp?"

"I found one, Coach."

"Hit some today, Yanks, my man?"

"Hit some, Coach," Yanks says, tears still in his eyes.

And Horgan sees an opening in the boys.

"Are you afraid to dive anymore, Sickopoose?"

"My mom plowed up a whole field, Coach. I dove all over it."

"Good boy."

"That calf get past you, Witherspoon?"

"No, sir."

"Hell of a lot of fun sliding into those chickens, hunh, Shrug, Pill?"

"Sure was, Coach," Shrugsby says.

Tending the species.

"Well, let's go get 'em," Horgan says, standing up, and his boys hit the blackened field at a run.

Horgan sits on the bench between Whit and the water cooler, placing his hands between the knees of his white, ash-smudged pants. He tells Whit about his dying father between pitches.

The Springtown leadoff man is a tall boy, with arms like needles. The bat looks like a fence post in his hands. He crouches, narrowing his strike zone, and Gaspar almost knocks his nose off with the first pitch. The boy leaps back and the weight of his bat carries him overboard and he finally falls a good six feet from the plate.

"What the hell?" the far coach yells.

Gaspar throws the next pitch a bit slower and over the plate and the boy hits a high fly ball into left field. Everyone stands. One of the Rutleys says, "Oh, oh, wait, wait," moving forward, moving back, moving forward, till he finally nestles in under the ball and catches it.

The tall boy, halfway to second base, dragging his bat, stops and begins to complain. "That guy almost killed me," he says. Then he tells his coach, "That pitcher almost killed me."

"Leave your bat at the plate. How many times I got to tell you?" his coach moans.

"I like my dad too," Whit says.

"I'm sorry you've had to sit on the bench so much this year."

"It's okay, Coach. I know the other guys are better than me. My dad still comes."

"So did my dad," Horgan tells him.

"Yeah?"

"Yeah. He was the coach."

"Oh."

Gaspar strikes out the next man on bad pitches. The far coach yells at the third man up to "Be a hitter." Horgan decides he will never use the phrase again.

But the boy becomes, and hits a sharp grounder between first and second base that Shrugsby dives for and misses. Right field Rutley scoops it up and tosses it in to Feeb, covering second. Pillsneck, on first, speaks to the ground audibly.

"Here we go," he says, and kicks at the red dirt. He signals a time out and races across the infield to Horgan. Horgan raises his arm and points back toward first before Pillsneck can say a word. As he recrosses the infield, back in front of Gaspar, Gaspar puts his hand and gloved hand on his hips, and then raises them to his ribs and then almost up to his armpits, in order to get his elbows out further and display the extent of his consternation with Pillsneck's lack of confidence.

Hey, batter, batter, Horgan thinks.

Cleanup is a thick boy, the Springtown pitcher. His father, the Springtown coach, sends him toward the plate with a pat on the butt. The boy, Chip, his father calls him, stands at the plate with a smile. He stands there taking practice swings while Horgan thinks, I have never once in seven years had a ballplayer named "Chip." Suddenly, while he stands there, the umpire himself rises up, calls play, and yells for Horgan. Chip drops his bat and raises his fists. So does Witherspoon. Horgan runs out of his dugout toward the plate. So does Chip's coach.

The umpire steps between the two boys and then steps between the two coaches. He says, "Now, we aren't going to have this kind of game, boys!" from behind his chest protector.

"What started it?" Horgan says.

"Coach, your catcher here told this batter he was going to kick his ass if he took one swing."

"My God," the far coach says. He says it again, "My God." Then he says, "You listen here, Coach, I'll kick your ass. What about teaching boys to play that way!"

"Shut up," Horgan says. "You're the fattest."

The far coach drops his jaw, spreads his arms and shows his belly pout again, turning to the umpire.

Horgan takes Witherspoon by the arm and drags him to the backstop.

"You gonna say anything like that again?"

"No, sir."

"Hunh?"

"No, sir."

"Okay."

They walk back to the plate and Horgan says, "He won't do it again. I'm sorry."

"Damn right you are," the far coach says, and turns back to his dugout, nodding all the way. At the gate he stops and looks up into the bleachers. He says, "We're gonna have to get back on the bus before this game is over. Mark my words." And he revolves back to the ball game.

Chip dominates the box, his man leads off first,

Gaspar goes into his stretch, and Horgan thinks, swing and I'll kick your ass you little shit.

Hey, batter, batter.

Hey, batter, batter.

The mothers of Eckley lean forward and clutch their hands.

"C'mon little Gasp!" they yell.

And the ball leaves his fingers.

And the ball is returned in the same direction it came from but fifteen feet higher, over Gaspar and over Sickopoose in center field, who dives straight up but to no avail. When he comes back to earth he must turn and run. There is no fence and the ball hits the ground and skids, rolls on the flatness, the barest resistance. It rolls and rolls.

Horgan watches it diminish, the ball in all its white purity, its perfect form, horsehide, cork, and string, leave him once again.

"I wish he wouldn't die too, Coach," Whit says. "But maybe he's tired. Maybe he'll go to heaven."

"He's awful tired," Horgan says.

"I was scared you wouldn't come, Coach. Shrugsby's grandpa told us your dad was sick."

"It's a funny thing," Horgan says, "he's dying, but you guys need me more than him."

Do you think, Horgan thinks, that he took me solely as an opportunity to get her? Yes, Horgan thinks, but not after the first two weeks in Eckley. Perhaps he took me because he knew he was unable. Never consummated. And never interested in anyone else. My virgin father.

Sickopoose overtakes the ball and throws it to Shrugsby, his cut-off, but the two runs are already on the bench. The ball comes in two slow arcs back to Gaspar. By the time it arrives he is in full tears.

His mother climbs down from the bleachers but stops at the fence when she sees Horgan on his way.

She yells, "It's all right, honey."

Gaspar's body is bent in the wind. Horgan puts the palm of one hand to the small of his back and with the other cups his salty cheek and bends him back up. Gaspar's hat is tilted off one corner of his head. It comes to this angle after the contortions of each pitch and he usually rearranges it immediately afterward. Horgan sets it straight for him.

"We never did get you a new hat this season, did we?"

Gaspar shakes his head and wipes his face with the back of his glove. "Maybe Pillsneck ought to pitch, Coach."

"What? You two have been switching off all season. Pillsneck pitched last week. Now you've got to hold up your end. It's your responsibility."

"I'm not a very responsible person, Coach."

"Sure you are, Gaspar. I saw you at the elevator today going after your father. That was a responsible thing."

"But he isn't here. He can't come."

"That doesn't matter. He knows where you are. My dad couldn't come either," Horgan says. And he says, "Hey, that ball you pitched at Miss Eckley's door. That was a strike. Throw at that tin door some more this afternoon, okay?"

"Okay, Coach," and Gaspar does not smile but he takes the home run ball in his hand again.

"Okay," Horgan says. It's Horgan that smiles. "There's still five innings after this one. We've got a long way to go."

If I am unable, he thinks, on the way back to his dugout. Do not think. There is the game. Don't fail in this, worrying on the other. A coach doesn't live or die on his long arm. I am trying to think what I am doing different now that I am of knowledge, now that I am born and unborn. Still waiting on a birth. Ha, ha, he thinks, unable: just and just atonement for my father's transgression. Hey, batter, batter.

Gaspar winds up and throws in the midst of a gust which takes his pitch, rolls and warms it, twists and expands; and the ball, off the fifth man's bat, pops up in a serene Horgan arc to Yanks at third. The fifth man turns around and faces the wind and Horgan, watching him, almost feels guilty. The wind whistles through the chain link with its hands in its pockets.

Popcorn, heated grain, blows across the charred ground, gaining grey.

Kidder pulls back the curtain, eyes forward for Horgan's father. She says, "Hi, Joe," but finds him asleep. She sits in the ready chair and leans forward over her purse, over her clinched knees, and kisses the old man on the ear. "Not to worry," she says, whispering. "There's an heir." And she sits back up after her whispering, her hand on his arm, and cries over the doctor's news. "You're the first person I've told," she cries.

Pillsneck, lead off, drives the first ball like a fire truck into left center for a double. Chip and Chip's father are equally incredulous. They both bear down, Chip's father on Chip, and Chip on the ball, and Rutley, Rutley, and Yanks fall to nine pitches. Pillsneck, picking up his glove and heading back for first, tells Horgan, "Curves, Coach, he threw ten curves that only broke half as much as mine do. Let's not lose, Coach; why do you want to lose?"

The cars of the Burlington-Northern clash, the

sound reaches Horgan a half-second later, and he jumps. The birds on the backstop jump too, one over another, changing places.

You know it would be so easy to give in to the fat man, Horgan thinks. That easy, and go home. Ten pitches. At least the inning was quick. See my father who is not my father and my wife who holds me up, hiding her desire. All hidden, hiding. Not me, not me, not me.

All the boys but the outfielders are to their positions when Horgan calls them back to the dugout.

"Get back on the bus, boys!" the far coach cries in response, "Get back on the bus!" But no one moves, not even the far coach.

The umpire, mask removed, stalks the cage of the dugout. "What is it, Horgan?"

"Just a little pep talk," he says.

"Time for that when your team's at bat."

"I know, I know," Horgan says, "but I forgot something."

"Well, let's get it over with and get back on the field. I won't have this procedure again."

"Yes, sir," Horgan says.

They crowd about him, caps tilted back, gloves jammed in armpits. "What'd you forget, Coach?" Sickopoose asks.

He drops to one knee and takes in as many boys as his arms will swallow. "I forgot to tell you I want to win," he says. "I'm always forgetting to tell you that. I want to win more than I've loved any dog I've ever had."

"It's okay, Coach," they say. "It's okay."

Horgan nods and leaves his head hanging. "I want to win bad," he mumbles.

"He's a poor thing," Shrugsby says.

"It's okay, Coach."

"Well," Horgan says.

"We better get back on the field, Coach," Witherspoon says. "We've got to go now."

"Sure," Horgan nods. "Yeah, y'all go on. I'm sorry."

The boys retake the field, and Horgan thinks, I have got to calm down. I need to do that. He sits between Whit and the cooler again. This place is so flat, he thinks. I never thought you could hide anything. I've never lost a baseball. But it's not that way at all. The earth curves. It's a ball too. Every step you take is an act of balance. We are all in the circus.

"Play ball!" the umpire cries.

And Gaspar throws two fine, quick strikeouts and Horgan thinks, well, that's all I had to do, ask, but the third boy knocks a triple down the right field line. The boy stands on third base, a few feet from Horgan, like a reproach.

"Blow me up like a balloon and let me go," Horgan mumbles.

"We'll get this next guy," the older Norblunk growls, and he pops his glove with his cast.

Man on third leads off, leads off, and Gaspar throws a strike on the inside corner. The infield stands up, makes tight circles in the red dirt, and bends back over. Man on third steps back off the bag and Gaspar, losing his cap, throws a ball wide and into the dirt. He is racing toward home plate before he's even through with the pitch. But Witherspoon shuffles to one side and digs it out, the ball a calf's nose. Man on third does a calf's step and returns to third. Witherspoon ladles the ball back to Gaspar. And from the stretch the third pitch is sent reeling, man on third leading off, and the batter meeting the ball evenly in a sharp line drive toward shortstop, toward Feeb, but high, higher than Feeb and his taut arm and fingers, so he lets go of the glove for a split second at the extent of his upward leap and it leaves his palm and becomes a body of water, and the ball catches there in the soft waves of leather and finger. He lets the glove drop back down onto his hand in an arc and looks into the pond of his pocket, the ball floating there, with wonder and joy. The batter, only half a step across home plate, drops his bat. Horgan's heart beats again before it can stop, and he slams the chain link with his hand and cries, "FEEB! FEEB!" Man on third does not get to go home, and the held and expelled air from the fans behind Horgan is audible above the land's wind. It raises the fine hair on the back of his neck, but he doesn't dare turn around. The eyes of Pillsneck's father.

"We'll get 'em next time around, boys," the Springtown coach bellows and he swats the rear of each of his team members as they take the field. He follows Chip to the mound, but only so he can be a bit closer to the Eckley dugout when he whispers over the wind to Chip, "Let's ease up a bit on them this inning." Then he turns full face to their dugout and yells at Feeb, "That was a fine catch, young man," and he winks.

"Get off the field, you dinosaur," Feeb screams.

Horgan bends over and examines his shoe laces as Feeb yells. Hmmm, he thinks, still tied. Better retie 'em.

"All right," the far coach cries, extending his arms in the position of crucifixion. "If that's the way y'all want to be. I can't help you.'' He turns back to Chip and says, ''Give 'em your stuff,'' and he staggers off the field, holding his palms out to the umpire and shaking his head sadly.

And it's true. Witherspoon manages a foul tip before he strikes out, ushering wind, wind among wind, but Sickopoose and Shrugsby only manage six pitches between them before the whole team has to give up the bench and assume the field. While his son pitches the far coach reads the back of a cereal box that blows up against his dugout. He scratches his cheek and yawns when his team comes off the diamond.

''Gosh, Dad,'' Chip says, ''you don't have to act like that. We've only got two runs.''

''Son, I know what's best. You sit down there.''

Springtown's first man thumps a ball over Feeb's head and it nestles into a loose patch of dirt. Before left field Rutley can dig it out the Springtown boy has limped to first. After he hit the ball he hit his own knee. Chip comes in to run for him. He stands on first with his hands on his hips.

''Your curve stinks,'' Pillsneck tells him.

''If you're so great why aren't you pitching?''

''Our coach doesn't want to win.''

''Sure,'' Chip says.

''He couldn't care less,'' Pillsneck asserts. ''You just watch. If you win it won't be because of your pitching.''

On the next pitch Pillsneck takes a smooth grounder and throws to second for the force out, but throws a smooth four feet over Shrugsby's head. The batter arrives safely at first and Chip moves on to third. Horgan calls time and moves out across the charred diamond for a mound conference. The infield comes in to meet him.

"Great pitch," Yanks says to Pillsneck. "You're one hell of a pitcher."

"Shut up," Pillsneck says. "It was just an error."

"All right," Horgan says, "all of you shut up, and listen. This boy on first is gonna try to steal second base. You're gonna throw him out, Witherspoon."

"But, Coach, this guy on third will score," Witherspoon says, lifting the stop sign of his mitt toward Chip.

"The wrong him," Horgan says, and he lowers his voice to a whisper, dragging the boys in. They listen, nodding, and walk back to their positions.

Gaspar's first pitch is wide, bringing Witherspoon out from behind the plate, but no one moves. The far coach smiles, and touches his peeking stomach, the brim of his cap, his left breast, and then licks his lower lip. Gaspar throws again and the man on first heads off for second. Witherspoon pockets the strike, jumps from behind the plate and throws, and at the same moment Chip heads in for home. But Witherspoon's throw doesn't go all the way to second. It goes to Feeb on the edge of the burnt infield, and Feeb has it back to him in time for Witherspoon to wedge himself behind himself and the spinning earth, in time to catch Chip. Chip tries to slide into Witherspoon's glove too, with the ball, and succeeds.

"Yer out!" the umpire cries, and rips the air with his thumb.

"Dad!" Chip cries, "Dad! You said to, Dad!"

"Yeah," Horgan sneers, "yeah."

The far coach plunders onto the field, his arms still crucified, his mouth receiving stones. "Isn't this

Little League?'' he cries, ''Aren't these kids playing here? What kind of underhanded ball are we teaching them?''

''This boy's out, Coach,'' the umpire says. ''You need to get him off the field.''

''Come on, son. Now we know who we're playing with.'' Chip follows his father off the field.

The second out of the Springtown third inning comes on a sharp line drive to Shrugsby. The third out comes when Shrugsby pretends to hand the ball back to Gaspar, but holds it in his glove instead, and walks back, whistling, to second. He waits there on the bag for Gaspar to wind up, and when the Springtown man leads off second base Shrugsby touches him, saying, ''Gotcha!'' This is when every man on the Springtown team and all of their fans join the coach by standing up and holding out their arms. They are like great birds drying their wings.

Bottom of the third.

Feeb strikes out.

Gaspar strikes out.

Pillsneck catches the ball on its torque and drives it down the third base line. It catches the corner of the bag and ricochets to Horgan's feet. He has to decide to move. The third baseman takes it, and throws hard to first, but over first and into his own dugout, where it knocks over three cups of water. By the time the first baseman has the ball Pillsneck is hard on his way to second. The first baseman throws over his coach's cries of ''Don't, don't,'' and throws wild, the ball wet and heavy, careening into center field and picking up an even coating of red dust and charred bits of grass.

''C'mon, c'mon,'' Horgan cries, and Pillsneck takes on third, and the ball—in the direction of third, yes, but a third on a higher plane—the ball, with a perfect boy's handprint affixed, flies over the dugout, causing the flight of birds, and drops onto the fender of Horgan's fire truck, leaving its dusty mark there. Pillsneck walks home, stepping on the plate almost ruefully.

"You're a hell of a pitcher," he says to Chip.

And the inning closes with a Rutley strikeout, the score two to one, Horgan thinking, the apocalypse is an hourly thing.

You know the evening is on its way here when the shadows become larger than life. The birds around the elevator try to flock with their shadows but can never catch up. The sun falls and falls, and the moon brightens in the blueness. People drop their visors, hide behind things. The coming of the evening seems an unbelievable promise. Who can believe it will be dark soon, after all this day? Who will buy a match?

Dutton, the grandfather, steps down out of the bleachers at Horgan's beckoning.

"You didn't tell me all of it," Horgan says.

"Your father asked me," Dutton says.

"I just wanted you to know that I know, all of it, and you don't have to worry anymore. I don't know how it affects me anyway. I don't know that it has anything to do with me."

"Okay, Horgan," Dutton says, and he stands there, the wind blowing him forward, his shadow pulling him back. "I loved you, always have, but at the time I loved your father more." And Dutton turns, saying "good luck," turning, to his truck, and Horgan lets him go.

And Ooper bats back the soil of his eyelids and rises, the silt falling and drifting back. His face is red with it. He rises, sitting up, so that only his head is above the rim of the ditch, rests on the level of the plain bodiless. And it turns, the eyes narrowing, narrowing, frightened but with purpose, with fore-sight. He sees the fruit of his love.

And the Springtown fourth falls, again, scoreless. Horgan does not have his beer. Whit's father brings forth his cooler and offers but Horgan says no.

"You don't think there are still any cinders floating around from these fires today, do you?" Whit asks.

"I doubt it," Horgan answers. "I wouldn't take these bleachers as any kind of a sign at all."

"I feel like I'm taking an awful chance by coming to watch my boy play ball."

"Better your lumberyard than your son," Horgan says. "I need to get him in the lineup." But by the time he turns around his team has already taken the field again.

"Three more strikeouts," Norblunk the younger tells him.

"I guess we've got to swing where the ball's not," Horgan says, "and hope it gets there."

"He's an awful good pitcher, isn't he, Coach?" young Whit asks. He shifts back, so his butt drops over the back edge of the bench.

"He is, but his arm will be useless by the time he's in high school. It'll be like a wet noodle. It'll be like a SpaghettiO on the wall," he says.

I don't believe that, he thinks, even if I am unable. I can only wait. I am tired of waiting. The bad thing about having a child is you thrust the responsibility of having a parent on it, without its asking for that.

"Okay," he yells, cupping his hands to his mouth, "let's not have any mental mistakes out there. Keep a head on your shoulders."

The team slaps their fists into their mitts in answer.

Gaspar settles his cap, rubbing the big E on it for luck, and throws. He throws his only pitch, a fastball, that becomes progressively slower as the game goes on. But so do the Springtown bats. And while they meet the ball consistently, pushing, pulling, Eckley just backs up, before and under every ball. Springtown has two men on base when right field Rutley backs under a high fly that the wind plays with, opens the maw of his glove as wide as it will, and catches the ball. He tosses in to Pillsneck, with two outs now and only a force play to hope for, but Pillsneck takes the ball and throws hard toward Shrugsby on second base and a Springtown runner late returning to the bag. The ball is a strike thrown at the open sky, but the far Rutley is able to run it down and hold the runners to second and third. Horgan steps out of the dugout, but steps back in a moment later. What to do with that boy?

"You'll go in this time, Whit," Horgan says.

"Which Rutley do you want me to go in for, Coach?"

"I want you to go in for Pillsneck."

"I've never played first base before."

"You haven't? Well, I'll put Rutley there and you play the outfield then."

"Okay."

"Okay."

When Horgan looks up Witherspoon is already three-quarters of the way toward first base, throwing down his mitt.

"Spoon!" Horgan yells, "Spoon, leave him alone!"

Pillsneck backs up.

"Get him, son!" Witherspoon's mother yells from the bleachers.

And he has Pillsneck in the dirt before Horgan or the umpire can get there. "You Dirty, you Dirty, you

Dirty," Witherspoon says, over and over, as they drag him off Pillsneck. "Coach," he yells, "I gave him one chance and he took two. The Dirty."

"Okay, okay," Horgan says, and he picks Witherspoon up into the sky by one arm, swats him once on the rear with the flat of his palm, and sets him off back toward home plate. Then he helps Pillsneck from the dirt.

"What happened to that fine arm of yours?" Horgan asks. Horgan holds him by the fine arm.

"Let go of my arm," Pillsneck says. "It's you who wants to lose."

Horgan lets go. He feels the scratches of his face, arms, and belly, his black eye, the bump on the back of his head, his bruised knee, his searing, smoke-filled eyes. "I don't want to lose. I'm just tired. Haven't you ever been tired?" he asks.

"No," Pillsneck answers.

On his way back to the dugout Horgan looks in the sky for signs of rain.

The third out of the Springtown fifth inning comes on a hard grounder to Shrugsby at second. He takes the ball on the run and keeps on running, not throwing to Pillsneck on first, but carrying it there himself, beating the batter by half a step.

And it is here, in the middle of the fifth inning, as Horgan makes his substitutions with the umpire (right field Rutley to first base and Whit to right), that his father dies. And the small sigh, the shred of wind, that Horgan sighs at this moment is indistinguishable from the others of the day. His father breathes, breathes, and does not. His body falls to the level of the land, becomes part of the flat horizon.

"You might have waited," Kidder whispers, tears coursing, all the air of the partition hers now. She calls and the nurse comes, and together they watch the flat line of the monitor.

Horgan gathers his next six batters. "Just swing. Swing as he pitches. He throws a hard curve and none of us have been able to hit it yet so just swing."

"Pillsneck hits it," Feeb says.

"Well, just hit it. We've only got this inning and next, okay? I've got Sickopoose, Shrugsby, Feeb, Gaspar, Pills . . . no, Rutley, and Rutley. That right?"

"Right, Coach."

"Okay, boys, this is it, try to hit the ball. It'll be a long, dry winter."

The bleachers, the dugouts, all rise as Sickopoose walks to the plate, fatherless.

"Pitch hardball, pitch big league," the far coach cries to his son.

Chip throws and throws a strike past the swinging bat of Sickopoose.

Cheers from the far bleachers, and from behind Horgan, in the home bleachers, someone yells, "Houses burning at a fine rate around here, yes."

Sickopoose swings again, swings hard, and falls in the red dust. He looks to Horgan and Horgan steps forward a step but then can only raise his unknowing arms. Sickopoose pushes himself back up, rubbing his throat.

A throw and he swings, misses.

"Yer out!" the umpire, a local god, screams.

And Sickopoose turns back to the dugout with sobs coming, and Horgan meets him halfway, bending down to one knee and taking him by his elbows.

"Stop," Horgan says, "Stop. Save it for something more important. Baseball, at any one moment, is a game of nine against one. There's no shame in being the one and losing. None. You hear me?"

Sickopoose runs his forearm under his nose.

"You hear me?" Horgan asks again.

He nods.

"Okay. Get back to the dugout and yell for Shrugsby."

"Swing where the ball could never be," Sickopoose tells Shrugsby as he passes.

And the stands rise for Shrugsby, and sit.

And the stands rise for Feeb, and sit.

"I would bat next inning," Pillsneck says. "You can put me back in when they come off the field."

"Hush," Horgan says.

Out on the Route you might drive right through this town without hint of lives turning. Driving west in the evening, the sun is orange in your eyes, things coming up out of nowhere. But the water on the road gone, the hundreds of miles of water on the road now gone, and the vertical things of the horizon reattaching themselves, that band of hazy blueness separating water tower from earth, telephone pole from earth, relinquishing now. In dusk there is some appeasement. It's an easy place for you to forget in. It's out of the heat.

Gaspar throws and the batter pulls up, bunts, but Witherspoon covers it like shell over yolk and throws him out.

Gaspar throws and the batter sweeps across the plate, picks the ball up out of the dirt and slides it toward Feeb, who waits there with the oiled scoop of his dustpan. He throws to Rutley too, and the home bleachers rise again, hope in their open mouths.

Gaspar throws, and Ooper, in the glare of the low and sinking sun, begins his ascent up the vertical and narrow ladder of Miss Eckley's elevator. He climbs with one hand, the other clenching the gas can. The steel of the ladder retains the heat of the day and burns his palm, but he climbs on, unseen. "I love, I love," he breathes, as he climbs.

Throws, and the ball, struck hard, climbs, climbs, and peaks, not catching the wind, and falls to young Whit. He moves beneath it, watching it as a bird across his backyard, and catches the ball as he would a sparrow, gently, and with awe, careful of its eye and wing.

"Yes!" Horgan cries, "Yes, yes!" and he waves his boys in. He is still one run behind.

The lights of the Dairy Mart blink, blink, and blink on. The manager comes to the front door and looks out upon the world.

Horgan's chickens swell about the backyard, the cock crows, and then they all go to roost.

The pumpman at Phillips 66 feels a pang of conscience and retapes his "GO ECKLEY" sign over his "Flats Fixed" sign. He puts his hands to his hips, looking across the Route, past the elevator and over the open land to the ballfield, its tiny figures, Gaspar walking to the plate. It's the pumpman that spots Ooper on top of the elevator, pouring the gasoline over his head, letting it flow down cooly over his dusty clothes.

Dutton walks into the tin office, bending down to get in the door, blocking all the light, saying, "Well, it's done now, Marian."

She saying, "You waited long enough, didn't you. He was a content, arrogant boy. He was doing fine."

"He had to know, Marian. Joe's dying and you and I will too, soon. He had a right to know."

"Then why didn't you tell him all of it?" She sits

behind the metal desk, looking up. She doesn't raise her voice.

"Joe asked me not to. I told him I wouldn't," Dutton says. The office ceiling is so low he has to tilt his head forward.

"Well, I told him something more. That was unfair of you, Dutty. You live with that now. That was your decision back there too. You loved Joe more than me. So it was you who gave him Horgan."

"It was both of us that gave him up. It was a good decision. He deserved him."

"I'll have you leave now. Don't come back."

"I won't, Marian."

"Don't," she asks.

"I won't," Dutton breathes.

"It was a sad little thing, wasn't it. Joe loving me and me loving you and you loving Joe. And now the poor boy to live with it."

Dutton sighs his deep sigh and says, "Horgan, of the four of us, will come out the best. Of our body, but he has Joe's heart."

Gaspar swings, snares a seam of the ball, and runs. All rise. He runs while the ball floats halfway to shortstop. The shortstop waits for it, glove down. But when the ball hits the ground it does so torqued and instead of rolling into the open glove it spins wildly and turns spinning, all that curve and wood-wrenched leather, and rolls back toward home plate. By the time the catcher traps the ball and throws, Gaspar is at rest on first base.

"My God, my God," the far coach yells, and calls for a check of the ball. "Something's been done to it," he screams, his spread arms encompassing all league infractions.

"It was your boy pitched the ball, Coach," the umpire tells him.

"Check the bat then," he says.

"That bat is hardwood, like any other," the umpire says. "But that boy of yours is throwing curves. He bought that piece of backspin."

"You mean to tell me you're going to call that a hit, and let the boy stay on base?"

"It was a hit, and he's safe on base."

The far coach turns to the field. "I guess we ought to load up right now, boys, and go home."

"You do that and you'll forfeit this game," the umpire tells him, banging his mask against his hip.

"Okay, Mr. God," the coach says, and on the way back to his dugout he points his finger at his son and says, "Throw nothing but perfect pitches from here on out."

And Chip nods, tightening his grip on the seams of the ball.

Right field Rutley comes to the plate, leaving his brother in the on-deck circle. He stands in the batter's box, and waits. Gaspar steps off first base, and becomes a stick man, ready to go in either direction. Rutley takes two straight strikes swinging and so Horgan begins to look toward the feigning Gaspar and touch his belly, pick his nose, rub his crotch, scratch his underarms. He signs to Gaspar on first, signing steal, steal, steal, steal on this pitch. And the pitch comes, and Gaspar throws himself into his running, Rutley swings, a miss, and the Springtown catcher, so used to the third pitch strikeout, rises and throws the ball around the horn instead of to second base. Rutley strikes out, but Gaspar stands tall on second base, safe after his slide, and the fans leave the bleachers, crowding down to the chain link fence. Their fingers stick through like hundreds of worms. Horgan moves out of the dugout to coach third base. He moves out with his thumbs in his armpits, flapping his elbows, clucking.

The far coach yells, "They won't steal home, son. Perfect pitches. Just six more."

And left field Rutley swings, and swings, and swings. He is out before Horgan has time to think. He consoles Rutley, who sits next to his struck out twin, and then Horgan thinks again and looks, and he looks, looking for a batter, and finally realizes it is Whit, who is sitting next to the water cooler with his hands on his belly. Pillsneck realizes too and intercepts Horgan on his way to Whit.

"You can put me back in," Pillsneck says. "He's been in for a full inning. You can put me back in. I'm two for two. Prove you want to win, Coach. Prove you don't want to lose. I can win it for us. I can hit that guy."

Horgan looks. He looks at his arm and then up in the bleachers.

The umpire looks into the dugout and says, "Need a batter, Horgan. It's true, what the boy says."

Whit, oblivious, holding a water cup up to a dry bird on the fence.

Horgan remembers losing a ball in the sun once and connects this with Whit, staunchly motionless at the plate all season, refusing or unable to take a swing. The boy clucks at the dry bird.

Miss Eckley screams at Ooper. She screams, "You come down here to me!" Ooper clings to the summit of the concrete canister, waving his box of matches. He opens a galvanized hatch and the dust of a bin boils thickly up around him. He steps down into the bin, down its ladder, and the men below, surrounding Miss Eckley, begin to run.

Dutton steps up behind her and says, "Let's go, Marian."

"Get away," she screams and she climbs up two flights of steel steps and enters the quarter-filled bin. The grain takes her in to the knees. The chaff and dust are so thick inside that she cannot see her own hand, much less Ooper, a hundred feet above. So she throws her voice at him, screaming, shaking her fist upward, "Come down here where I can see you, goddammit! Come down here and fight me! Take me on! You can't do anything to me!" And she screams upward, knee deep in food, rage, rage. "Not me!" she curses, gasping.

"Okay," Horgan says, "Okay. Whit, you're up." All right. I've said it. It's done, he thinks.

The boy turns and looks, holding his cup, looks at Horgan and the umpire, and then to Pillsneck beneath them both. He says, "Coach, you can let Pillsneck play."

The fans, the ball team, the umpire, the far coach, the mothers, scant fathers, turn as the leaves of a tree struck by wind—to Horgan.

Christ, he thinks, Christ. "Don't you want to bat?" Horgan asks.

"Yeah, but..."

"No buts. It's your turn. Find you a bat and helmet and get out there."

"NO!" Pillsneck screams, and his father reaches grasping through the chain link at Horgan. Even Whit's father gasps.

"Houses burning down like crazy," someone else behind him says.

Horgan moves back out to coach third base and

behind him the boys begin to chant. They chant for Whit, who leans over the plate and returns to them his broad butt, the back of his folded ears.

"Hard now," the far coach coaches his son, "the best you've got."

He throws, a fine hard curve that starts high and speeds up as it drops into the strike zone. Whit stands so still as it goes by that Horgan wonders if he even breathes.

"C'mon, son," Whit's father yells, and the rest of the crowd takes note of him.

They murmur, "That's his father."

The second pitch starts way outside and twists coming in, sliding over the inside corner.

"Strike two!" the umpire yells, and does not even bother to click his counter over.

It is finished, Horgan thinks. Perhaps I have waited too long, just a bit too long. He watches Whit at the plate, and watches a bird, a crow, descend and settle on the tip of the boy's upraised and perfectly motionless bat. The crowd titters, and finally guffaws. Whit turns his round head slowly up and notes the bird, and he smiles. And Horgan thinks, this is the life I have been waiting for. My God. I love my days. And then he does not know what to think, and finally he thinks that the thing to think is that life is what happens while you are waiting for something else. He feels the sun on the back of his neck. And hears a familiar sound, the slamming of Kidder's car door, so he turns in that direction and watches her walk toward him, in all her beauty, alternately raising and bowing her head, and he lets go a sob for his father, and feels that watching her walk across this field is enough, all his life's knowing and unknowing balled up into one moment, his understanding that by nightfall each day became the coming, and the last judgment. It was such a hard thing to learn, to look at the world from a father's point of view, rather than a son's.

He takes her in his arms and she says, "You're okay. You're okay, Horgan. You're going to be a father. It's okay."

"Yes," he says, holding her, and the game holding for them. "Yes," he says, "I've been trying to deal with that today." He stops, and looks out across the ballfield, at the boys standing out in the burnt fields. "We're all perched on the edge of the world out here, aren't we?" he says.

"Yes, honey."

"I'm not unhappy about it."

"No."

"I am so proud," he says. And then again, "I am so proud." And he suddenly realizes he will have to, in some way, offer Miss Eckley his father's house, a bed for the night. He lets Kidder drop down off her tiptoes, out of his arms, to stand at his side. He drapes his arm across her shoulders as they turn to watch Whit, and he says, "Well, here we are at a ball game." And he waves at the umpire to continue.

The umpire pulls his mask back down over his face and Whit and his crow steady themselves, wait on the perfect pitch.

"Play ball!"

"I hope he hits a homer," Kidder whispers, looking up at Horgan, squeezing his hardened hand.

And Horgan says, "Yes, me too."

And as Whit swings, and the crow takes flight, Ooper speaks gently, sadly, to the world, saying, "I love," and strikes his match, but before he can set himself ablaze, consummate, he and the dust and the Eckley Elevator, all, explode.

And over Eckley Field and over Horgan, who has tears in his eyes for Kidder and the baby and his father, and over the seventy-five running men, running behind them a huge old man carrying a screaming old woman who in their struggle almost seem to be dancing, and over and across Eckley and for miles around this flat place, the grain falls. And through this falling, the birds rising and going back to the fields, Pillsneck's repentance, and through this falling the caroling of children, and then the radio waves saying the world's weather is changing and that there will be rain soon and again and again and Kidder saying, "I'll bet," and Horgan adding, "Yeah, don't hold your breath," but when the winter comes he is rubbing oil over her swelling belly, and the oats are three feet tall at Eckley Field and for miles, miles—oats sprouting and growing from window boxes and rain gutters, cracks in the sidewalks, the ruins of Miss Eckley's elevator, and a single shoot of oats from the seam of Whit's home run ball, never found, lost somehow, but perfect and secure and pure in this far, flat place.